THE CAT AMONG US

THE CAT AMONG US

LOUISE CARSON

Doug Whiteway, Editor

Signature
EDITIONS

Cover design by Doowah Design.
Cover icons courtesy of Noun Project.

This book was printed on Ancient Forest Friendly paper.
Printed and bound in Canada by Hignell Book Printing Inc.

We acknowledge the support of the Canada Council for the Arts and the Manitoba Arts Council for our publishing program.

Library and Archives Canada Cataloguing in Publication

Carson, Louise, 1957-, author
    The cat among us / Louise Carson.

Issued in print and electronic formats.
ISBN 978-1-77324-015-2 (softcover).
--ISBN 978-1-77324-016-9 (EPUB)

    I. Title.

PS8605.A7775C38 2017   C813'.6   C2017-904696-9
                                               C2017-904697-7

Signature Editions
P.O. Box 206, RPO Corydon, Winnipeg, Manitoba, R3M 3S7
www.signature-editions.com

For Chanel and Aiden,
special friends

CONTENTS

PART 1

CATS

In the dim early morning light, she padded noiselessly from room to room. Other cats, draped on sofas, tables, chairs, followed her with their eyes, their necks swivelling lazily.

She was smaller than most of them, with petite features and stubby paws — a calico longhair — the favourite.

At the cat flap First Cat paused, whiskers twitching. She'd come to the contraption late, didn't like it, but had reluctantly conceded its usefulness.

A black shape leapt over her, butting the flap with its shoulder and was through. The flap, a rectangle of flexible carpet, cut from the dining room rug and nailed above the back door's cutout, retracted, snapping First Cat on her nose. She blinked, then pushed.

Pausing on the narrow, grey-painted deck that hugged the back wall of the house, First Cat surveyed the world.

Below the deck, another level: a pink flagstone and mortar path also followed the contour of the building, led to asphalt on the left where the woman kept her car, and on the right to an enclosed back porch. Only the most favoured few were invited into this sanctum. Something about floor-to-ceiling screens and claws.

Perennials threatened to take over the stone path, sending small volunteers to root in its cracks. First Cat sniffed delicately at a clump of alyssum as she made her way from wood over stone to the slightly damp soil under a hydrangea bush. Her spot.

Four white feet glowed against dark earth. The black cat rolled from side to side, revealing the three white diamond patches that narrowed and widened from just under his chin to his belly.

Second Cat. He knew she was there. She hunkered down, made herself a small, compact watcher.

She knew why he had so quickly become a favourite. Whereas she had come as an adult to the house and had had to work hard to be loved among so many, Second Cat had arrived as a three-month-old kitten. That had been a bitter winter for First Cat, listening and watching as the woman bonded with Second Cat.

Now that he was four years old, he'd lost the advantage of kittenhood, but still possessed something First Cat knew she'd never had, something prized by the woman: a sense of humour.

He showed it now by turning his rear to her and kicking up a token few crumbs of earth. First Cat sprang, clouting one of his hips. He took off, darting out from under the hydrangea onto the lawn, to blink in the light and crouch, fair game for the swooping swallows. First Cat ignored his predicament.

The lawn stretched down a ways till it stopped by a strip of wild flowers. The woman didn't bother much with these plants. She concentrated on those closest to the house, where she grew herbs and vegetables and flowers for her bouquets.

Beyond the wild flowers were the rocks and pebbles of the beach. Not much for First Cat down there, though, on a hot day, there was something pleasant to her in lying on a shade-cooled rock, listening to the lake caress the shore.

The lake, the outermost edge of First Cat's world, where she knew she'd never venture.

An ant trundled by, towing a fragment of leaf. First Cat dozed. She was aware of half a dozen other feline forms in the garden besides those of herself and Second Cat.

To her left, somewhere below the asphalt and the car, but before the thicket that led to an abandoned house, she could hear

Mother purring as she groomed a half-grown cat held between her paws. Mother was one of the few cats whose given name was the same as her real one. Mother was Mother. Anyone, including the woman, could see that.

On the beach, three black-and-grey-striped tigers blended and unblended with the stones, as they worked out their complicated relationship during a game of catch the butterfly. Brothers, their positions within their own hierarchy continuously shifted, though within that of the house, they were fairly close to the top. The woman called them "the boys." It seemed appropriate to First Cat.

The only other cat she sensed nearby was the one the woman called "Stupid," because of his habit of suddenly biting or scratching her hand. A slim, shorthaired grey male, the other cats knew him not as Stupid but as Defiance, and gave him a wide berth. First Cat had heard the woman say of Defiance that he not only had no sense of humour, but he had a maliciousness to him, that he was an incorrigible.

First Cat wandered out from under her bush and sat at the edge of the lawn. The swallows wouldn't bother her there. No sign of Second Cat. She was wondering why breakfast was so late when she heard a dismal yowl from inside the house, then another. As she pushed through the cat flap into the dining room, she saw the others were uneasy: shifting positions, grooming.

She passed from the dining room into the hallway and froze as another yowl filled the house. Second Cat leapt ahead of her. She followed him, slowly hopped up the stairs towards the woman's bedroom. Second Cat, stiff-legged, skittered sideways back out into the hall, his short black hairs as puffed as possible. He stood aside as First Cat slowly entered the room.

The woman lay in her bed, unmoving. There was a strong smell. First Cat wrinkled her nose, then jumped on the bed to her spot on the right near the woman's side.

Instead of warmth and the rhythm of the woman, expanding and contracting regularly like the lapping of the waves on the shore, there was absence. First Cat curled into her usual place and waited.

1

The lawyer's voice droned on. "And to my nephew, Andrew Petherbridge, I leave my Royal Doulton, the Hummels and the other objects from my collection of porcelain."

Gerry opened one eye, sneaked a peak at her cousin Andrew, who was, she supposed, trying to look pleased, and closed the eye, resettling into her doze.

The train ride from Toronto, the drive to Lovering in the rented car, settling in at Fieldcrest, Cathy Stribling's big old bed and breakfast, were part of yesterday's blur. Today's included breakfast with Cathy and other guests, Aunt Maggie's funeral and interment, lunch at the Parsley Inn with the family, and now the reading of the will at Andrew's house.

Gerry suppressed a smile as she imagined Aunt Maggie's delicate figurines arranged throughout Andrew's place. Not that Andrew wasn't as conservative in his taste as the porcelain — he was — but he went more toward simple heavy leather and wood furniture, as evidenced by the pieces in his living room. The brass barometer on the wall was the room's single ornament. What had Aunt Maggie been thinking?

The lawyer continued with his list of bequests. "To Prudence Crick, I leave the sum of ten thousand dollars, in thanks for her service and her friendship." Who the heck was Prudence Crick? Gerry opened her eyes to see if she could pick her out from the ten people who were sitting in Andrew's living room. She thought she knew most of them. Probably Prudence was that stoic-looking fiftyish woman sitting on one of the kitchen chairs at the back of the room. The others were turning towards her with half-smiles and nods. Evidently, the amount was approved. Gerry became somnolent again, reflecting on what she'd left behind in Toronto — what? — just yesterday morning?

Her landlady had been kind but firm. "You have three months' notice and, I'm sorry, but I'm getting on and need my son and his girlfriend close by, so they'll be moving in after you leave."

After four years, that was it. She'd moved into that apartment when she turned twenty-one, a year before her dad died. Practically the only legal way to eject a tenant, a good tenant, was to have family move in.

She should look at it as a plus. A chance to move on to a better place. She groaned inwardly. Three months. And rents in Toronto so high. And she'd have to pay first and last months' rent. Maybe Aunt Maggie had left her a bit of money. That would help with the move.

"And to my niece, Geraldine Coneybear, I leave my house, The Maples, and all the contents therein, except those previously mentioned, as well as the sum of fifty thousand dollars, to assist her in its maintenance."

Gerry jerked upright and both her eyes snapped open. Andrew was shaking her hand as the other relatives crowded around. "Wow, Gerry! Fantastic! Good for you." Andrew really had a very nice smile. Too bad they were cousins. And how come he'd taken all the tall genes?

"Yes, Gerry. Lucky you." This smile not so nice. Margaret, Andrew's older sister, named for their aunt, loomed, her three glum-looking sons flanking her. Had she hoped to inherit? Gerry had no more than a second to get the impression of grinding teeth before her Aunt Mary, Aunt Maggie's sister and Margaret's mother, replaced her.

"Gerry!" She threw her arms around her niece, then held her at arm's length. "More like Deborah every day! The poor thing. She was so glamorous, your mother. That red hair and creamy skin, although she did have a tendency to freckle. And that fabulous figure." Here she raked Gerry head to toe with a critical glance. "It's been a while, hasn't it? Of course, dear Gerald's funeral."

Gerry flinched, thinking of that sad day when they buried her father near her mother.

"Is it really three years?" her aunt continued. "And now Maggie. It's just me left, isn't it?" She laughed.

Her husband, Geoff Petherbridge, looked embarrassed, but then, Gerry reflected, he'd had a lot of practice. "How are you, Gerry? Good to see you." He pecked her on the cheek. "Are you surprised to be Maggie's heir?"

"Totally, Uncle Geoff," replied Gerry, rubbing at the lipstick she knew Aunt Mary had pressed onto the side of her nose. She leaned forward and, under her breath, asked, "Did I get it all?"

Unfortunately, her query coincided with a lull in the general conversation. Geoff looked surprised and was beginning his reply, "Well, you heard the other bequests — " when Margaret interrupted her father with a cold edge to her voice.

"Weren't you paying attention, Gerry? You get it all. Everything. The house, land, furniture. The paintings." She seemed to choke on this last word and everyone stood still, waiting.

Gerry, now fumbling for a tissue in her pocket, replied, "I meant the lipstick Auntie left on my nose. Have I removed all of it?" She turned to Andrew, hopeful of a friendly response.

He gravely examined both sides of the nose before saying, "Clear."

Gerry silently mouthed, "Take me away."

Andrew smiled. "Why don't I bring you back to the bed and breakfast, Gerry? It's a lot to take in and you must be tired."

The lawyer stepped forward. "Miss Coneybear, my card. When you have a moment, there are arrangements, conditions we must discuss."

Gerry took the card. Cecil Muxworthy. She looked up, way up. Another giant. "Thank you, Mr. Muxworthy. I'll call later today if that's all right. I should get back to Toronto soon." With a vague wave and a general, "Goodbye," she backed out of the room.

As she passed an open doorway on her way to the front door, Gerry glanced into the room and was stunned to see shelves full of china figurines. To Andrew, she remarked, "So, you're a collector." He smiled and nodded.

As they stepped onto the narrow strip of land next to the ditch and a car passed close by, Andrew pushed her ahead of him. "Single file."

"I'd forgotten how hard it is to walk on the side of the road here." She impishly looked up at him. "Aren't you worried about leaving Margaret at your place? She may be jealous of your barometer."

Andrew made a face. "They'll let themselves out. We all have keys to each other's houses. Margaret is just…disappointed. She'd have loved living at The Maples. You remember what a great house it is."

They turned and looked at the long yellow building across the road from Andrew's more modest cottage.

"I'll have to sell it, I'm afraid." Gerry brightened up. With the money from The Maples, maybe she could stop renting and stick a toe into the ocean that was the Toronto real estate market. "I've got my work and my friends…" Her voice petered out, then she cheered up. "It'll be amazing to have money." She hastily amended her expression. "I mean, I'd rather Aunt Maggie was still alive, but — "

"But you're glad you've benefitted. Don't be embarrassed. It's natural to be pleased." After a pause Andrew added, "It will change your life."

"And you, Andrew, are the Royal Doultons and the Hummels going to change your life?"

Andrew laughed. "Serves me right. I always admired them in front of her. She loved them so. Actually, I do collect ceramics and Aunt Maggie's will round out my collection."

"Well, there are certainly enough of them, if I remember correctly. Her mother started collecting them, didn't she?"

"I think our Grandfather Coneybear presented the first one to his wife in 1938 when your father was born."

"Sweet. You're lucky, Andrew, both your parents are alive."

"I know. It was just bad luck your mother getting cancer so young, Gerry. And your father was — what? — fortyish when you were born?"

"Just forty. We almost share the same birthdate, four days apart." Gerry grew pensive, remembering her namesake father and her mother, buried in the same little churchyard where they'd left Aunt Maggie that morning.

They'd reached the drive leading to Fieldcrest, and Gerry said, "If you don't mind, Andrew, I'll go in and have a rest. See you later, maybe." He left her there with a cousinly kiss.

Gerry studied the large square building with its wraparound roofed veranda, wondered if she could incorporate it in any of her work. Its outline loomed the larger as it was set on a slight rise. The roof overhang brought the proportions down a bit and the veranda grounded the entire edifice. It was a monstrosity but kind of fun. Gerry took out her sketch pad and pencil from her purse and did a quick study.

Yes. It could be whimsical if she exaggerated the roof, there, like a hat, and pulled the walls in a bit like a waist. The veranda could flare out like a skirt. She hastily closed the pad when she observed her hostess, Cathy, yoo-hooing from the veranda. "Tea-time, Gerry! Tea-time!"

Gerry sighed and went up the stairs, looking at her feet. She just wanted to be alone. She changed her attitude when she saw the spread Cathy had prepared.

A plate of sandwiches, with their crusts removed, cut into triangles, squares and fingers. Not just scones, but three types of scones: currant, cranberry lemon and—Gerry's eyes widened—chocolate chip. Thick cream mounded in a bowl, butter, three types of jam, honey, and a lemon loaf, thinly sliced. Drool formed in Gerry's mouth as she eagerly sat down in a tatty old wicker chair that creaked every time she moved.

This, then, was the reason for Cathy Stribling's sturdy figure, though Gerry knew the woman worked hard enough that she deserved a skinnier one. She'd seen her that morning from her bedroom window, digging in one of her gardens, later walking her dog, and, even later, when she was sure all her guests were awake and fed, cutting the immense lawn with a small electric lawnmower and a complicated series of connected extension cords. She seemed to be thriving, a genuinely happy person.

Gerry heard Cathy's dog, toenails clicking on the wooden floor, moving towards the veranda. He rested his head on Gerry's lap, soaked her navy blue skirt with drool, and collapsed with a groan on the mat by the door.

Gerry took a sandwich and a scone and was given a cup of black tea, perfectly brewed. She leaned back against the wicker chair's cushions and sighed. "Cathy, you really shouldn't have."

"Well, I don't usually offer my guests quite as high a tea as this one, but you've had a hard day, so, I thought...no, Charles. Si-t. Wai-t." Her dog, a fat basset with something else mixed in — spaniel? setter? something with wavy hair—sat and waited, then, as exhaustion overcame greed, sank back down. Gerry dropped a crumb of scone near his nose and watched as he snuffled and eventually found it.

"I see you love animals," said Cathy, demolishing a stack of chicken sandwiches, "as I do." She began on the ham.

Gerry quickly helped herself to a cheese and pickle. "Well, not so much love as like." She reached down to pat Charles. "They're nice, I guess."

"Oh, my dear, I don't know what I'd do without Prince Charles."

Gerry's eyebrows automatically lifted on hearing the dog's full name. Obviously, Cathy either didn't realize or care how odd this sounded. "It's very lonely here when there aren't any guests."

Cathy was older than Gerry's cousins Margaret and Andrew, in her fifties. Gerry didn't know her that well, whether she'd ever been married, for example, and wasn't in the mood for exchanging personal confidences. She could use some information though. "How is the old house — The Maples? Is it still in good shape?"

"Oh, your aunt kept it as well as she could. It's the wood, you know." Here Cathy looked around at her own walls and floors, rather helplessly, Gerry thought. "I do what absolutely needs to be done," she continued. "The roof, the plumbing. But don't go down into the basement, my dear." She shuddered. "You don't want to know."

Before her eyebrows could lift again, Gerry reminded herself that Cathy was probably referring to mould or dust or spiders, not skeletons, and asked for another cup of tea. She took a slice of the lemon loaf and almost fainted. Still warm!

Cathy went on: "In the winter, when there aren't any guests — and I believe your aunt did this too — I close doors and just heat a few rooms for me. Sometimes" — here she laughed — "I've had to thaw the plumbing with my hair dryer."

Gerry laughed politely and thought of her soon-to-be-vacated apartment in Toronto, complete with a landlady who handled all the repairs and maintenance. Oh, well, she'd just have to find another. She sighed and put down her cup. "Is it all right if I go for a nap?"

"Of course, dear, you must be exhausted. It was a lovely funeral, though. Your room's all made up."

Gerry stood. "Can I use your phone? A local call," she reassured when Cathy began to look worried. She added sadly, "There's no one in Toronto I need to call."

2

Gerry swore as she swerved to avoid the woman pushing the black baby carriage along the winding river road. Her own fault; she'd been looking at houses, remembering which ones her parents' friends had lived in, which ones she'd visited to play with other children. The woman, with her neutral clothing, had blended with the road. If not for the carriage…and Gerry shuddered, thinking of the carriage, its occupant and the woman all flying through the air.

"It didn't happen. It didn't happen," she muttered and pulled into the parking pad next to The Maples. Look at that view. It must be worth millions. Waterfront doubled the value of a property. For the first time she felt a bit awestruck that her aunt had given her all this.

She was still sitting in the car, clutching the steering wheel, when Cecil Muxworthy ("call me Cece") arrived. He peered in at her. "You look a bit pale. Are you all right?"

Gerry got out and confessed. "I almost hit a woman and a baby on the road coming here. I'm still a bit shaky."

"That's terrible." His eyes twinkled as he added, "But there's no baby involved." When Gerry looked confused, he added, "You didn't recognize Prudence, your aunt's cleaner?" Gerry shook her head. "Prudence doesn't drive, and she always says the only reason she's still alive is because she doesn't walk anywhere without her carriage." He added, "It seems she's been proved right. Unfortunate."

"Why unfortunate? I didn't hit her."

"I just thought you'd maybe want her to continue to clean the house."

"Oh, yes, I see. You mean keep it nice for potential buyers to look at. Well, maybe she didn't notice me in the car. It's a rental."

"Yes, well. That's not important right now. I have to tell you some of the conditions your aunt laid out when she left you the house. Shall we?" He indicated an old picnic table in some shade at the side of the backyard. "It's a lovely view. Perhaps we could conduct our meeting here, then go inside after."

Gerry preceded him down the stone steps onto the lawn and plunked herself at the table. "It's so quiet, you don't really hear the road. I could get used to this." She stretched her arms and turned her attention to the lawyer, thin and homely but with a pleasant expression, in his early fifties, she estimated.

Cece shot her a quick look before explaining. "It's because the lawn is below road level and the house absorbs a lot of the noise. Not that it's a noisy road." He took her aunt's will from his pocket, unfolded it and laid it on the table before them. Behind him Gerry saw a small tri-colour cat sitting composedly on the deck above them.

"Did my aunt have a cat?" she asked. "Because that one looks like it owns the place." The cat lowered its front end until it was lying like a sphinx, staring at Gerry and Cece.

"Mm. Ah. Yes. She had a few. She had a few cats."

"I remember one or two when I was little and we visited, but they always ran away from me." Gerry became aware of some rustling behind her, turned in time to see a grey form melt into the raspberry canes. "How few?" she asked.

"Prudence says twenty, but I've never seen them all together to make a count. But she would know."

Gerry whistled in amazement. "Twenty! Boy, it must be hairy in there." She looked in trepidation at the house. "Is the furniture all torn up?" she asked anxiously.

"We'll go inside in a moment and you can see for yourself. My, my, look at the time. My wife will be expecting me shortly." He cleared his throat. "These are the conditions of your aunt's bequest to you. 'My home and its contents…previously mentioned…' Here we are. '…on the condition that she inhabit the house,'" Gerry groaned. "'for a period of not less than five years consecutively,'" Gerry sat upright. "'and that she cherish,'" Gerry groaned again. "'my dear companions: Marigold, Bob, Mother, Winston, Franklin, Joseph, Blackie, Whitey, Runt, Mouse, Stupid, Kitty-Cat, Harley, Max, Lightning, Jinx, Cocoon, Min-Min, Monkey and Ronald.'" The lawyer counted. "Yup. Twenty. Cats."

Gerry's voice was muffled as she rested her face on her arms on the table. "Ronald?" she asked faintly.

"Ronald." Cece produced a set of keys and slid them across the table. "Want me to come in with you?"

Gerry took the keys. "Do you know the house? Like where the electrical is and so forth?"

"Yes. But Prudence knows it best."

"Okay, then. I guess you can go. Thanks. Thanks for your help." They shook hands and Cece drove away.

Gerry sat back down at the picnic table and looked at the lake. Mature trees, mostly maples, framed her view. The water was still and the sky was blue. She turned her head to see the little cat still staring. As Gerry rose, the cat rose too, stretched its little back and yawned. Gerry walked to the side door, read Yale on the lock, and inserted the likeliest key. A match. She entered a little square porch, just big enough for an old bureau and a recycling tub. Some of her aunt's boots and shoes were still there, tidily lined up.

Gerry paused and gave a moment to remembering her father's youngest sister. A tall, happy woman, she'd never married, been content to live a quiet country life, walking the short distance to her church where her ancestors (and some of Gerry's) were buried, working in her garden. Not a bad life, Gerry supposed.

She unlocked the kitchen door with the next key on the bunch and stepped inside. The calico cat darted in almost between her feet, making her stop.

The kitchen was much as she remembered it, except for the footbath-sized container of kibble under the small table. The floor and counters were neat and clean. She stepped into the next room, the winter living room, her aunt had called it, where a giant ancient hearth dominated. A rectangular table with six straight-backed chairs filled the river-view side, while a couple of rockers stood in front of the fireplace. On the street side of the room was a long cushioned bench Gerry lay on when she was a child.

This was the room she remembered most from Christmas visits with her parents — where they would eat and warm themselves, where her aunt had her Christmas tree. "Too many ghosts," she murmured, and walked through a narrow passageway lined with cupboards full of china and crystalware. It felt strange to think all this stuff was hers. Back in Toronto she had the remnants of a cheap set of dinnerware she'd bought when she left home, as well as the odds and ends she'd accumulated. But this, this spoke of generations. She stepped into the large formal dining room.

Finally, some more cats. Around the edges of the room, against its walls, were pulled out the dozen chairs that went with the massive mahogany table. Over each chair's upholstery was draped a towel. And most of the chairs displayed at least one cat. It was a bit eerie.

As the cats registered Gerry, some of them sat up. One, a large marmalade tiger, left the chair she shared with a small white cat and came up to Gerry, rubbed against her legs. The little calico who'd been accompanying Gerry walked over to the tiger. The tiger moved away.

"Oh, you're the boss, are you?" Gerry addressed the calico. As the kitchen and winter living room had been, the dining room was spotless. The room leading off of the dining room, which Gerry remembered as a study, had been turned into a display area for her aunt's ceramic collection. Gerry flicked the light switch and gasped. Lights inside the cases, which lined the walls, illuminated hundreds, possibly thousands, of china figurines: Andrew's inheritance. As she looked at the various groupings — ladies in long colourful skirts, rabbits, children in shorts gazing winsomely — Gerry shuddered. Not her cup of tea. Andrew was welcome to them.

She returned to the dark dining room and opened the blinds on the windows overlooking the lake, then turned and counted the cats. Twelve, including the little bossy one. The others must be elsewhere in the house or outside. She moved into the spacious entranceway — as big as a room — and remembered why she loved it.

To her right was the front door with its small covered porch. On her left was the wide staircase leading up to a landing with a view of the lake. The staircase split to the left and to the right at the landing, then turned again to finish upstairs on a narrow balcony above her head. She hugged herself. It was hers!

A long narrow washroom was tucked behind the staircase and she went to check it. As she pushed on the partially open door, her nose told her she'd found the cats' toilet or, rather, toilets. Six litter boxes stretched from the doorway to the toilet itself. A cloth bag of plastic bags hung from a nail on the inside of the door. She selected one and scooped. Yuck. One of the downsides to cat ownership. She set the bag outside a door that led to the screened back porch. The sleek grey cat she'd caught just an impression of earlier darted in. Gerry could see where he or someone had been plucking at the screen door with sharp claws. She wondered if cats, like dogs, needed their nails trimmed.

Back in the entranceway, she turned left, entered her favourite room in the house, and the farthest from the kitchen. Known as the summer living room, it had been shut up in winter as too difficult to heat, but during the other seasons was, she suspected, her aunt's favourite as well.

Here were the books, lovingly protected behind glass-fronted bookcases, and prints and paintings displayed against the delicate pale green walls. From waist height down, the walls were lined with golden bamboo. The whole room had a sort of oriental-Impressionist flavour.

The artist in Gerry expanded. If she moved that sofa down there, and rolled up the carpet, here was a room in which she could draw and paint. She was relieved to note an absence of towels on the light green upholstery that covered the white painted banquette built in along two of the walls. She guessed that because of the wallpaper, most cats were forbidden the room.

"Except you, of course," she said to the calico who had softly followed her in and who she was getting used to having at her heels. "You're dogging me, you know." Bad taste, the cat blinked. "Sorry," said Gerry. They went out of the room and upstairs.

Five bedrooms for the family, separated by a partition from the servants' bedrooms where a narrow second staircase led down to the winter living room. "I forgot about that." She pushed on the partition. It opened easily, led to the modern bathroom, an office and a couple of small rooms being used for storage. "Well, of course Aunt Maggie didn't want to go down then up again to go pee in the night." The cat watched Gerry as she inspected the tub and sink, ran the taps briefly, and looked out the window.

There was Andrew, standing in his garden across the road, looking at the house. Gerry stepped back. He must have been the one Aunt Maggie turned to when she needed assistance or advice. Someone to change a fuse when the lights went out. Gerry shivered at the thought of winter in the house if the electricity failed. "Oh, no," she said, looking down at the driveway to her right. Someone was pulling in.

"I'd have been here earlier but some maniac tried to run me off the road. I was so upset I had to go tell Mother." Prudence Crick set out twenty small plates on the kitchen counter. She opened four large cans of cat food, then removed some plastic containers from a shopping bag she'd brought and opened them up, showing the contents to Gerry. The kitchen door was shut but Gerry was aware of a furry multitude mewing and pushing at its far side.

"Chopped cooked chicken — dark meat — and chopped cooked chicken livers. For Madame. She's got hyperthyroidism and can't eat the regular stuff. Won't touch kibble." At Gerry's wide-eyed look, she smiled grimly. "You'll get used to it. You eat chicken?"

"Yes," Gerry murmured faintly, wondering if Prudence was offering her a portion of the chopped meat.

"So when you cook some for yourself, you just cook extra for her, eh?"

Gerry was about to admit she rarely cooked when Prudence jerked her head in the direction of the small cat, the only one allowed in the kitchen during meal preparation, apparently, who was passively awaiting the presentation of her food.

Prudence continued, "Just don't salt it. It's the salt that revs up the thyroid. I know. I had to cook salt-free for Mother for years." She began to set the plates on the floor. Gerry passed the remainder to her and was stooping to add the plate of chopped chicken and liver to the rest when Prudence stopped her. "That one goes there." She pointed to the top of the fridge.

"Well, obviously," Gerry joked. No response from Prudence, but the little cat jumped from floor to chair, to counter to fridge top. Gerry meekly put the dish in front of her. Prudence opened the kitchen door.

Nineteen varicoloured bodies rushed in, found a spot and began eating voraciously. Prudence pointed them out, telling their names. "That big marmalade is Mother because she's motherly.

She's one of the biggest, so easy to recognize. Those three grey tigers are the boys — Winnie, Frank and Joe — they're brothers."

"Who's the little white one near Mother?"

"That's Ronald."

Gerry bent over and stroked the thin back. The little cat shivered and continued eating. "Pleased to meet you, Ronald."

"He's Mother's latest and the last one to arrive here."

"Her latest?"

"Her latest adopted child. She'll look after him until he's grown and settles in." Sure enough, Mother had been unable to finish her plate of food, had made room for Ronald to gobble it up. Prudence then rattled off the same list of names Gerry had just heard enumerated in her aunt's will. Prudence concluded by looking at the top of the fridge where the little calico was cleaning her whiskers with her paws. "And that is Marigold — Top Cat." The cat paused in her grooming to acknowledge the sound of her name, then resumed her licking. Prudence added, picking up empty plates and filling the sink with soapy water, "But I call her Madame, don't I, Madame?"

Some of the other cats shifted their attention to the tub of kibble while others wandered back into the house. Gerry, bemused by all the activity and trying to put names to various hairy faces, only half heard Prudence, then snapped to attention. "…every Monday and Thursday from nine to three with a short break for lunch. Of course until you move in, I'll come every day, feed them and clean the boxes. Forty dollars regular and ten just to do the cats."

Gerry calculated rapidly and made a decision. "Could we just do once a week cleaning and of course cat feeding when I'm away, which I will be…" Gerry spoke slowly, with the dawning realization that what she was saying was really going to happen "…until I pack up my Toronto apartment and move…" She gulped. "…move here."

Prudence eyed her keenly, let the water out of the sink and grabbed the mop, which she wet under the tap. "Make a nice change for you, Miss, going from a city apartment to a house with a garden. And it's not as if you're a stranger."

"Call me Gerry, please. And may I call you Prudence?"

"You may." She finished her mopping, rinsed the mop in the sink and returned it to its corner. "Will I come back tomorrow or Thursday to clean?"

"Thursday."

"I'll need a bit of money for Madame's meat."

"Of course. How much do I owe you? My purse is in the car."

Prudence took an old flat black purse off the counter and led the way out the side door to the parking pad. There, parked next to Gerry's bright red rental, was the black baby carriage.

Gerry found herself walking the upstairs hall between the family's bedrooms and the servants', the thin white kitten clasped in her arms. She was wearing her favourite soft white nightgown. A low moon illuminated the hall with its slanted light. She pushed the partition gently and slowly it opened. She heard her mother's low, drugged voice call her name, and entered the little white room where she lay. The ceiling was steeply angled either side of the window where the head of her mother's narrow bed was placed. Gerry laid the white kitten down on her mother's chest. Her mother turned her head, opened her mouth and —

"*Gerreee. Breakfaaaast.*" Gerry took a sudden breath and returned, blinking the tears from her eyes. She sat up in the spacious bedroom Cathy had given her.

The day before, after Prudence had left The Maples, Gerry had contemplated sleeping there and had returned upstairs to examine the bedrooms more closely.

The largest, her aunt's, had been tidied, but her clothes remained in the closet and drawers, and the presence of four unblinking cats grouped on the end of her bed had made her uneasy. A black longhair, a pale beige longhair, a grey and white shorthair and a small grey tiger were lying where Gerry imagined her aunt's feet would have lain. "The honour guard, eh?" When Marigold jumped up, circled, then lay close to the pillow on one side, Gerry got the picture. Why, these cats are grieving, she thought, and left them to it. She'd decided to sleep at the B&B.

Getting out of the double bed and crossing to the window, Gerry looked at the lake. Another beautiful day. And she had to get back to Toronto. She hurriedly showered, dressed and packed. Over blueberry pancakes with maple syrup, she quizzed Cathy about the cats. "You used to visit Aunt Maggie, right?" Cathy nodded, her mouth full of French vanilla coffee. "So what did she do with the kittens? I mean, all those cats…" Her voice trailed off as a vision of Maggie handing newborns over to Prudence to be disposed of creeped her out.

Cathy swallowed. "Oh, that was one of her rules. She only took in cats that were fixed, or she paid for them to be fixed right away. No, Maggie knew there were enough unwanted cats in the world without wanting to add to their number. But as her older cats died, she'd adopt a young cat, sometimes a kitten. Bob, Ronald, the boys — they were babies when she got them."

"I haven't yet met Bob but I know the others." She forked more pancakes off the serving platter. "Why Ronald?"

"Did you get a look at his face? He's got a thin black moustache below his nose. So, Ronald Colman." Gerry looked blank. "The actor. *A Tale of Two Cities.* He plays the hero."

Gerry mumbled, "I'll have to look him up."

Cathy put on a faint British accent. "'It is a far, far better thing I do than I have ever done.'"

"That's a lot of pressure to put on a little cat."

Cathy laughed. "You have a sense of humour, like your aunt. I remember when she named him. We laughed and laughed. Even Prudence cracked a grin."

"You were close to my aunt?"

"Not close close. We were neighbours. She liked having people over for tea or for a swim in the summer. Speaking of which, have you used the pool yet?"

"I didn't even get down to that part of the property. I've been trying to come to grips with the house and the cats. I'm still amazed she left it all to me. Why did she, do you think?"

Cathy poured them some more coffee. "Well, she knew Mary didn't need it — Geoff's got that fabulous house at the other end of town. And Mary's not the person to leave in charge of anything living, much less a house full of cats. Those children of hers brought themselves up, or went to their father."

"That explains why Margaret's the way she is, but how did Andrew turn out so nice?"

"Oh, I don't know — girls and their mothers, I suppose. And Andrew has had his difficulties. He takes after Geoff." She sipped her coffee. "But back to your original question. No doubt Margaret would have liked The Maples. It would have meant a step up from that little house at Hill's Corner. Or for one of her sons. But I don't think Maggie would have thought Margaret would cherish the cats, and the boys — " She laughed. "The boys have a bit of growing yet to do."

"How old are they?"

"Well, she had them one after another — three in four years. Maggie used to call them 'the litter.'" Cathy sighed. "I'll miss her." Then she cheered. "But now you'll come and live here and I'll get to know you better."

Gerry smiled sweetly. "I'm looking forward to it, Cathy. The boys?"

"Oh, yes. They're late teens, early twenties, I should think. Yes, Margaret married young. And then to that awful Douglas Shapland."

"I noticed he wasn't around much, just turned up at the funeral lunch, had a few drinks and left."

"I saw that too. He'll wind up in a ditch one night, you see if I'm right." She spoke vehemently and Gerry was surprised.

"Why, Cathy, you sound as if you hate him!"

Cathy rose and began stacking their dishes. "Not hate. I just feel, what a waste. He was so talented and now, nothing. Just a drunk. You see him on his bicycle, wobbling to the bar, then wobbling home." She smiled at Gerry. "I used to babysit him and I remember what an adorable little boy he was. Such a shame. Are you ready to check out, dear?"

Gerry settled her bill and put her suitcase in the car. As she drove past The Maples, she looked for signs of life. There weren't any except for the baby carriage at the side door — Prudence was feeding the cats.

3

Gerry took a towel, sunglasses and a sketchpad and called over her shoulder, "I'm going to Yalta."

Prudence yelled back, "Fine," and returned to her work.

Gerry, in her swimsuit and a pair of flip-flops, happily walked down the stone steps and breathed the sweet air wafting from the garden. She'd missed the heavenly scent of apple blossoms for this year, but the roses were in first bloom. She paused and lowered her nose to one. She remembered her father had known their names — Madame this and le Duc de that — aristocrats all, mostly old varieties. The vegetable garden her aunt had planted that spring was coming along. She wondered who was weeding it.

Having Prudence come once a week hadn't worked. Gerry hadn't realized what a lot of work such a big house required. And she needed Prudence's help as she sorted through Aunt Maggie's stuff. So Prudence came Mondays, Wednesdays and Fridays.

She'd been living at the house for a few weeks and was loving it. The two weeks in Toronto had passed in a blur of packing and explanations to her employers and friends. Some of the employers had agreed to her continuing to work for them, some had not. She wasn't worried. She thought she could pick up new freelance art assignments without too much trouble.

Her friends had been disbelieving, then enthusiastic. "Darling, of course we'll come and visit you. It sounds wonderful." "Of course, I'll have to take massive amounts of decongestants. Well, the cats, you know, and my allergies." "We'll definitely visit. You're so lucky."

And Gerry, laying out her towel on the chaise longue by the pool and settling in the morning sun with a sigh, did feel lucky. Except — the cats.

She was used to the daily feeding now and to the cleanup after. The litter boxes were gross, though most of the cats had made the seasonal transition to using the garden some of the time. Prudence changed the towels on chairs and the bedding once a week, did the laundry, vacuumed, dusted, so the house was clean. Gerry was sleeping in a bedroom at the front of the house, left her aunt's room to the cats. She closed her door at night with a feeling of relief.

It was just that — well, they hadn't taken to her. She said hello, she fed them, she wondered if any of the longhairs were getting tangled fur. (Prudence had shown her the basket of combs and brushes kept on the little bureau on the kitchen porch. "Your aunt used to put them up on that and groom them. Most of them love it.") The nicer, more passive ones allowed her to pick them up; Mother even purred. But none of them sought her out. Marigold no longer followed her about the house as during her first visit, but slept on her aunt's bed at night, sat under a hydrangea bush all day, was growing thin.

At least by the pool Gerry had the boys around her. Winnie, Frank and Joe. It was their spot. They loved the water, stalked the ripples Gerry made when she swam or floated, batting at them with curious paws, came close to falling in. They were friendly enough but, having each other, didn't really need her.

She closed her eyes and lay on her back, her ears partially submerged. The pool was close to the lake, which was part of the Ottawa River. She could hear the odd motorboat in the distance, the drone of a plane, the breeze in the willow that overhung the pool, the birds, the — *splash!* She dropped her feet and came to attention, treading water. "Which one of you — ? Oh!"

The boys were as astonished as she. It was the black cat, a short hair with white boots, throat and whiskers, who was foolishly swimming from side to side, trying to claw his way up the concrete sides of the pool. A spray of willow leaves floated nearby.

Gerry swam gently over and, putting one hand on the top edge of the pool, used the other to sweep under the black cat's body. His swimming back legs raked her skin and she changed her plan, grabbing him by the scruff of the neck and lifting him to safety. "Ouch, mister, you got me good," she exclaimed ruefully, examining her damaged forearm. The cat shook like a wet dog, then began grooming. "Bob?" she said tentatively. He was the only black cat among the group with such distinctive white markings. He gave a friendly meow and came over to be petted. "Well, you're a nice one. Good thing it's warm. Go find yourself a patch of sun." As if paying attention, Bob flopped by the side of the pool that was in full sunlight, regarding Gerry with large round yellow eyes.

The boys jumped around Bob, asking for a game, but he wasn't to be distracted. Gerry got out of the water, dried off, put on her sunglasses and lay down on her back with her knees bent. She squawked when something wet and furry passed underneath them, kneaded her wet towel, circled, and made itself at home. Now I'm stuck, she thought, as a faint purring came from Bob, but all the same, she felt faintly pleased.

She must have dozed off because she woke to the backing up beep of a truck. Bob leapt into the ivy that surrounded the pool. "What the — ?" she muttered and went up to the house to see.

Prudence was giving the driver of a cube van directions as he positioned the truck in the semicircular driveway, stopping him when the van's rear door was lined up with the house's front door. Andrew got out of the driver's seat and smiled at Gerry. She'd wrapped her wet towel around her shoulders and was shivering in a patch of shade. "You look about ten years old," he said.

She made a rude face. "Thanks. What are you doing?"

"I know, living across the road, I could have taken the ceramics bit by bit, but I thought I'd be less of a bother if I took them all at once."

"Of course. I'll help you pack them. Can you help too, Prudence? Just let me get dressed." She tore off up the staircase, threw on some shorts and a t-shirt and tied back her hair. She met Prudence and Andrew in the dining room. Andrew had brought a lot of empty boxes from the liquor store. Gerry opened one. "Brilliant, Andrew, they have separators for the bottles."

"Yes, I thought that would work for the ladies. Of course we'll have to wrap the smaller pieces individually." He flushed. "I suppose you think this is a strange hobby for a man."

Gerry replied smoothly, as they made their way into the room where the figurines glistened, "Not at all. I expect it was an interest you picked up from Aunt Maggie."

Andrew brightened. "That's it. She loved her pieces. Some of them are very old." He lifted one off its shelf and reverently placed it in the box. "I made the shelves for her."

"Oh, aren't you handy!" exclaimed Gerry. "Are they built-ins?" She stepped closer to a case to examine it.

"No. They're free-standing. But I bracketed them to the walls just in case." He gestured back into the dining room. "Cats leaping about and so on."

"Then you must have them. The cases, I mean, not the cats. I'm not allowed to give them away. Not that I want to," she added hastily. "I have a plan for this room and it'll be bigger without all the display cases up against the walls. Take them."

Andrew glowed. "Well, if you're sure. They match the ones I made for my own collection. Thank you."

They worked hard the rest of the morning and early afternoon, and by late afternoon Andrew was gone and the room was empty. Prudence offered to clean it, but Gerry said she'd do it herself and sent her home. The room would need more than a cleaning before it was ready for what Gerry had in mind.

She changed into a little sundress — green polka dots on white — and a pair of comfy sandals, tucked a ten- and five-dollar bill in the little clutch purse that held her key, and set off on the short walk to Cathy's. Not being much of a cook but liking good food, Gerry had fallen into the once- or twice-weekly habit of dining with the owner of the B&B. And, as Cathy didn't have many guests during the week, Gerry was almost always able to indulge in a cozy chat with her hostess.

She walked around back of Fieldcrest and knocked at the kitchen door. A cheerful "Come in!" and the sound of running water let her know dinner preparations had begun.

Charles lay between sink and stove. His tail whacked the floor but he didn't get up. Cathy patiently stepped over or around him. "It's so hot, I thought a beautiful salad followed by strawberry shortcake." Gerry groaned. "Do you have a pain?" Cathy asked.

"No, but I'm starting to get a bulge." Gerry patted her stomach.

Cathy laughed. "That's nothing. Wait till you're my age. Bulges all over."

As she'd spent all day with him, the topic, naturally, was Andrew. "How'd he come out so nice from that awful family?" Gerry asked, spearing a green bean, a bit of hard-boiled egg and a cherry tomato on her fork.

Cathy drank her chilled white wine. "Mm. So good. Andrew is the exception that proves the rule. And your Uncle Geoff isn't awful, just put upon."

"Put upon?"

"Well, Margaret and the boys live in one of his family's houses and he pays for everything, including the boys' educations and athletics. They eat almost every night at the yacht club or the golf club restaurant."

"Do they ever eat here?"

Cathy sniffed. "I'm fussy about who I eat with, so not everyone knows they can get a good supper here without being a sleepover guest." She cast a furtive glance over her shoulder, perhaps seeing the taxman waiting to pounce. "It's cash, so the fewer who know, the better. Andrew comes sometimes."

"That reminds me." Gerry took the money she'd brought and slid it across the table. "Is that enough?"

Cathy examined the bills, rose and put them in a drawer. "Thanks. But back to Andrew. You know by now he's got a house full of ceramics."

"Yeah, but he almost didn't want to admit it. Does he think it's effeminate?"

"Well, it is, dear. But whereas Maggie mainly maintained the family collection, Andrew buys every new piece the companies put out and he's always looking for older pieces. Besides the choir and his work, I think it's all he's interested in." She dropped half a hard-boiled egg on the floor. Charles swam over and ate it lying down.

"He still works with Uncle Geoff at the furniture company?"

"Yes. Their showroom is in town. Not my style."

Gerry looked around the kitchen. By the look of it, nothing new had entered that room in the last twenty years. There was a pause as they happily continued eating.

"You never told me, really, why you think Aunt Maggie left me the house. It wasn't just to spite Mary and Margaret. She could have left it to Andrew."

"Andrew's got a house and it's paid for. No —" She poured Gerry another glass of wine. "I think it was because you're your father's daughter."

"Dad?"

"Yes. Maggie probably thought it was right Gerald's daughter got something. She got the house almost by default. Gerald had moved away. Mary was well taken care of by Geoff. Maggie was still living at home when her mother passed away."

"Gramma Ellie. She was only fifty-five. A lot of us seem to die in our fifties," Gerry mused.

"Yes, but look at your great-aunts Sylvia and Mary. In their eighties, nineties."

"They were Catfords."

"Well, you're part Catford." Cathy put more salad on Gerry's plate. "And Maggie knew you were an artist. She loved the arts. Used to draw herself, when she was younger."

"I did not know that."

"So she thought—I'm just guessing—you'd appreciate the house and its location and not mess around with it."

"Mess around?"

"You've seen them—former cottages with new top stories and weird frontages added on. Or the owners just let the old house decay until it's uninhabitable, tear it down and build some modern horror."

"Is that what's happening with the abandoned house to the north of mine?"

"I think so."

"Not all modern houses are horrible, Cathy." Gerry offered Charles an anchovy. He heroically half-rose and slobbered into her palm. She hastily grabbed her napkin. "Slimy," she told him. He wagged his tail, licked his chops, and lay down again.

"No, but you know what I mean. How are you and the cats getting along?"

"Funny you should mention it. Just today one of them cozied up to me. Of course, I'd just saved his life and he was cold and wet, but still. The black and white one—Bob."

"Oh, Maggie loved Bob. He didn't sleep with her. Marigold was jealous. But he kept her amused. Always ready to play. Maggie said he was safe, had soft paws."

"Prudence warned me about two cats. A big grey named Stupid and a strange, mostly black calico with a stump of a tail named Lightning."

"Yes, I didn't see them too much. They were the difficult ones. Even Maggie had to be wary around them. Not counting Marigold, the gentlest ones were the four who slept on her bed. They were quite social. Most of the other ones would run away when people visited."

"Not Mother."

"No, not Mother. But Mother was always too busy mothering her latest to bother much with humans. I'll get the dessert."

After a first and second helping of Cathy's strawberry shortcake — freshly baked biscuits, split, stuffed with cream and luscious local strawberries, the top half rakishly atilt with a topping of more cream, a single perfect berry and a mint leaf — Gerry staggered home, checked the cats and cat boxes and went to sleep.

She must have taken a tad too much wine, because she slept through till just before nine, was still in her sleeping shorts and T, drinking her first coffee when Prudence arrived. "I'm going to go through Aunt's clothes today, Prudence. Is that something you could help me with?"

Prudence nodded. "Before or after my regular work?"

"Oh, after. I have some work I need to do." Gerry poured herself another coffee and wandered into her studio, the bamboo room, as she always thought of the summer living room. A drop cloth covered half of the floor. Her art table was set up in the west-facing window and was littered with brushes, paints, crayons, computer. She studied her work.

Her bread and butter was her comic strip that had been running for about two years. *Mug the Bug* was a success, in one national and a few provincial papers. She hoped someday to collect the strips in a book. For now she was committed to five a week. She'd found the easiest way to generate material was to construct a narrative and follow it along rather than trying for resolution every day.

Mug was just a dot on the page. It was in his context that Gerry got to show off her illustrative skills. For some reason *Mug* had been in the desert recently, so she had been having fun with cacti and distant mesas. But it was time to move on. She imagined him out of the desert and onto the deck of an ocean liner. Perhaps the ocean liner would lose power and descend into a chaos of unwashed and underfed guests for a few days. Gerry had never liked the idea of a cruise: stuck out there with hundreds of strangers. She drew.

A slight scratching noise outside the door made her pause. It stopped. She went back to work. The scratching resumed. "Oh, for heaven's sake!" She threw down her pencil and opened the door. Her voice softened. "Oh, hello, sweetie. How are you?" Marigold, thinner than Gerry would have believed she could have become in only a month, came noiselessly into the room. On impulse, Gerry picked her up and was surprised when she felt the cat relax against her. She went over to the banquette and sat down. Marigold turned a bit, mewing, then settled, attempting a weak purr.

Gerry stroked her. "Poor thing," she murmured. "Poor thing." As the cat slept, Gerry relaxed against the back of the banquette, let her gaze range around the room. She leaned to reach the bookcase to her right, pulled out a book at random. Small, slender, blue, printed in 1934: *The De Coverley Papers from The Spectator*. She had read a few chapters when she got to the first illustration. Now she was really interested. She looked at the pen and ink drawing of Sir Roger being greeted by four of his old and faithful servants and an old dog not unlike Cathy's Prince Charles, and marvelled at the subtle facial expressions. Muttering "line, line," she rose, put the cat down on a cushion and went to her desk. She spent the next two hours trying to emulate an artist dead before she was born.

She felt fur against her ankle and realized she was hungry. She knew the cat was. Prudence had subsequently revealed that while nineteen of the cats were content with the twice daily meat-feed and subsequent kibble-grazing, Madame Marigold's condition meant she was fed, or at least offered food, five or six times a day.

Gerry could hear Prudence vacuuming above their heads as she poked in the refrigerator. She offered the cat a plate of chopped chicken and made herself a sandwich of the same. The vacuum cleaner stopped and Gerry yelled, "Prudence, do you want lunch?" When Prudence declined the offer, Gerry took her sandwich, a banana and lemonade, and went to sit on the screened back porch. "I'll never take this for granted," she muttered to herself, settling on a rickety metal chair at a rickety metal and glass table facing the lake.

By now, the Virginia creeper had climbed up the walls to the porch's roof, enclosing the room in green. Small birds cloaked themselves in the creeper's thick privacy. Gerry looked at the lake.

"I'm finished," Prudence said, joining her with her own lunch.

"Prudence, who's been clipping the creeper? Come to that, who's been weeding the garden? And cutting the lawn? It can't be you."

"Now, when would I have time to do that?" Prudence replied, biting into the peanut butter and pickle sandwich with potato chips that was her inevitable meal. She swallowed, drank some lemonade. "He's a private guy, at least with his family. It's your Cousin Margaret's husband, ex-husband, I mean, Doug. He liked to do it for Maggie and she'd give him money from time to time."

"Money to get drunk on?"

"Maybe. Sometimes. But otherwise, money for art supplies. He's an artist like you."

Gerry sat back, open-mouthed. "Nobody told me. Another artist in the family. I'd like to meet him." She gestured at her backyard. "I must owe him a big pile of money by now. Will you tell him I'd like to pay him?"

"Tell him yourself," said Prudence, placidly chewing and nodding down toward the shore where a man had just beached a canoe. He was of medium height and build, looked to be in his early forties.

Gerry stood up and gestured. "Hey, Douglas. Doug. Come have a drink," and stopped, appalled at what she'd just said. "Prudence, I didn't mean — I mean — "

Prudence kept eating. "Just get him a lemonade." Gerry rushed to the kitchen and back and found Doug sitting and chatting with Prudence. A shy smile filled his pleasant face and he stuck out a hand. "Pleased to meet you, Gerry. Again, that is, now you're all grown up. Thanks." He drank the lemonade in one draft. "Well, this is nice."

They fell silent.

"How are the — " "How are you — " "The tomatoes are — " All three stopped and laughed. Doug said, "I can guess what Prudence was going to say. 'The tomatoes are really coming along.' Right?"

Prudence nodded.

"And I was going to say 'How are you settling in?' But I can see you're settling in just fine."

"I am. I love it. I was going to ask how the boys are?" Gerry added hastily, "And Margaret, of course."

Doug replied easily. "I don't see much of Margaret. The boys I meet at the yacht club. I work on refitting boats for owners — scraping, painting, maintenance."

Gerry wondered where he lived. "So how are they?"

He grinned. "Getting into the usual trouble boys get into. Cars, boats, motorcycles. And girls. And beer." Knowing his history, Gerry didn't know where to look. "I'm clean, Gerry. I go to AA at the church hall. Maggie knew. She was great. Always my friend."

Gerry replied softly, "I'm so glad, Doug." Then, jumping up, "What do I owe you for all the work on the lawn and garden?"

As she went into the house to get her purse, she heard Prudence and Doug explode with laughter. Nice to have people in the house, she thought. And another part of her plan, for the room that formerly housed her aunt's ceramics, fell into place.

4

It had taken two hours, but Gerry and Prudence had turned out every drawer, as well as the wardrobe, in Maggie's room. Blackie, Whitey, Mouse and Runt had sat on the bed while Marigold supervised from Aunt Maggie's pillow. Of the three piles — throw away, give away, and keep — the middle one was by far the largest. Maggie had kept her clothing in good shape, and Gerry made it clear to Prudence that she was to have first pick of the giveaways.

Gerry herself was gaga over the collection of vintage purses, though she couldn't see herself ever wearing the Victorian ones. Meant to be hung at one's waist, they were balloon-shaped or pendulous sacks, their embroidery or beadwork in now-unfashionable and faded colours, with heavy metal clasps and gold tassels. "These belong in a museum."

Prudence responded primly, "They belonged to the family."

Gerry rewrapped them and turned with delight to those of the early twentieth century. She sat on the bed near Marigold and exhibited the purses one by one. "What do you think of this, Princess?" The cat seemed to accept the title, though possibly thought it a trifle junior, as her eyes blinked at the shiny objects. "This is Art Nouveau and French. And this. And this." Gerry looked at the delicate silver and gold purses on her lap. "These are art," she added, in an awestruck tone.

"Well, get some use out of them," urged Prudence. "No point in keeping them wrapped up out of sight." She picked up a suede concoction with a striking serpent clasp. "This is interesting."

"That," announced Gerry, taking the purse and reverently laying it down, "is Lalique." She picked up two more: a black beaded clutch she estimated to be from the 1950s, and one from the 1920s, flat, silver and gold glass-beaded, with a chain handle. "I might use these. They seem to be in good shape."

She helped Prudence take the bags of garbage or donations down to the front hallway. "I'll drop the donations at the rummage sale," said Gerry. Prudence had a few things for herself in one bag. "Can I give you a lift, Prudence?"

"I'll be fine."

Gerry followed as Prudence carried her bag to where her baby carriage waited at the side door, next to the little red Mini Gerry had bought — her first car.

"Don't forget, you haven't even looked in the garage yet."

Gerry moaned. "This'll take forever." Then she cheered up, remembered she was going out to dinner with Andrew that night. No cooking. "I'll just take a quick look, get an idea of what's in there."

Prudence slung the bag into the carriage and set off toward home.

When she turned back toward the house, Gerry almost tripped over Bob, who'd gaily dashed between her feet, then flopped on the driveway, presenting his tummy. She rubbed it and the cat gently closed four paws and his open mouth on her hand. "Oh, Bob, you're so much fun!" Gerry looked up to see Marigold's pinched little face before the cat disappeared under the hydrangeas. "Oh dear. Oh dear, Bob. Jealousy."

She fetched the key for the garage from the board hung in the little side porch off the kitchen. Many of the keys were untagged. She shrugged. Probably Prudence would know their various uses. Or Doug.

This key was clearly marked "garage" on a bit of masking tape stuck to it, so Gerry confidently approached the padlock on the long low shed-like building's wide doors. She pushed back the hasp and opened both of them up as far as they could go.

She'd been allowed to explore in it when she was little, and it hadn't much changed. Old garden implements hung from the walls. A canoe was suspended in the roof, resting on two rafters. Maybe she could get Doug to help her bring it down.

Bob had followed her into the garage and was sniffing around. "Hey, Bob, wanna go canoeing with me?" The cat sneezed and began grooming. "Dusty, eh?" Gerry sneezed too and the cat paused to give her a look before resuming its licking.

Gerry pushed between old scratched bureaus and lamps without shades to the other side of the building. One whole wall was taken up by a big piece of plywood resting on the floor. She peeked behind it and her eyes lit up.

She walked the wood outside, reversed it, and, as it was beginning to rain, quickly carried it back inside and leaned it against the wall. She stood back a little to get a better look.

It was a family tree. Someone had first printed in pencil, then painted over, to record members of the Coneybear family for generations, beginning in the early nineteenth century. It must have been done some time ago, as none of the more recent deaths — those of her mother, father, grandmother, Aunt Maggie — were filled in.

She was reminded that her grandmother's maiden name was Catford. "Cat ford, Bob. Get it? The place where cats cross water. You found one the other day when you fell in the pool."

But Bob was fixed on a point across the lawn and his tail was twitching. Gerry assumed he was tracking a bird and turned back to her genealogy. "Let's see. We have Coneybears, obviously, and Petherbridge, Shapland. Oh look, a Parsley. I didn't know I was related to the restaurant. Oh, rats! I better get ready. Bob — "

There was a snarl and Bob was across the lawn as Stupid dropped from the largest maple. Grey fur and black tangled together, then Stupid drew back, ears flat and one paw raised.

"Bob!" shrieked Gerry, not wanting to lose her favourite — or see him hideously disfigured.

Stupid obviously hadn't known she was there, and slunk away. Bob sat at the foot of the maple and groomed. When she went over to check, he seemed intact. "Oh, you guys," she said, chucking him under the chin.

Upstairs in her room, she pondered her reflection in the full-length mirror. In the front of the house, the room hadn't proven noisy. She lived on a quiet road, even though, twice a day, people left Lovering and returned to it, for work or for appointments elsewhere.

The room was square with a high wooden bed and matching wardrobe. She'd cleared away the ancient bedding and the lace mats on the bedside table and vanity, and replaced them with her own simple pale green sheets and coverlet, leaving the tabletops bare. She'd also gotten rid of the ratty old carpet. She liked looking at the wood floors, painted a dull brown.

The mirror was painted the same colour. She considered painting it white, then concentrated on her appearance. Little black dress. Check. Wedge-heeled black sandals. Check. Vintage gold-beaded purse with fringe. Keys, money. Check, check, check.

She smiled at the little redhead in the mirror. Good enough, she thought cheerfully. Away I go.

She drove to the Parsley Inn and Restaurant. The last time she'd been there had been for Aunt Maggie's wake. She'd had the fish and resolved to be more adventurous this time.

A bored teenaged boy waved her into the parking lot. It was nearly full. She was impressed. She pulled in next to Andrew's car. He must have arrived just ahead of her.

It's nice of him to invite me out, she thought, but maybe I'll pay for myself, just to keep things simple. Or I could offer to pay for him next time.

Another teenager, a girl, slightly more gracious, welcomed her at reception. "I'm meeting Mr. Petherbridge." The teenager nodded and gestured toward the dining room door to Gerry's right. As she turned, she looked to the left, where noisy laughter indicated the pub section of the inn, and saw Doug Shapland, wearing a plaid shirt and shorts, throw his head back and join in the fun. There was a drink on the table in front of him. As Gerry looked away, he caught sight of her and half rose, but she'd entered the dining room.

Feeling worried — had he fallen off the wagon? — surely a pub wasn't a good place for a recovering alcoholic — she stepped into a whole other ambiance.

A guitar was being strummed quietly in one corner while a large tank full of gold fish burbled. Hushed conversations were being conducted by nicely dressed customers who cast furtive glances in her direction.

The inevitable teenager approached. At least there were jobs for these kids locally. Gerry spied Andrew, half-rising from his chair. "There's my table," she told the girl and breezed over.

He'd managed to snag a window table, which was nice, but less nice was the fact that his sister Margaret and her three sons were already seated there.

Stifling a sigh, Gerry put on a smile and made the rounds, kissing Margaret and Andrew, and shaking hands with the boys: James, twenty; Geoff, eighteen, and named for his grandfather; and David, seventeen. She caught James looking down her dress front as she leaned over to seat herself. She stifled another sigh and turned to Andrew. "So, Andrew, how nice you invited some of your family." She smiled a sharklike smile at him. He looked slightly apologetic.

"Your family, too, Gerry," Margaret tartly responded.

"Of course you are, Margaret. Are Aunt Mary and Uncle Geoff joining us as well?" Gerry craned her neck, wondering if her aunt and uncle were about to appear.

Andrew smiled. "No, no. Mother and Dad have a function elsewhere. And I thought, as Margaret was on her own, that it might be a nice chance for you to get to know each other better." His voice trailed away as he looked from woman to woman, one glaring, one forcing a smile.

They were saved by their waitress bringing the menus, filling water glasses. The adults ordered drinks. To Gerry's surprise the two eldest boys ordered beer. She'd forgotten Quebec's drinking age was eighteen. She felt sorry for David, sitting with a soft drink while his brothers sneered.

She thought of their father in the pub side of the inn and was surprised again that their mother allowed them to drink in her presence. She must be put off by the whole idea. But no, Margaret enjoyed her martini, swiftly dispatching it and ordering another.

Gerry studied the menu. "A Caesar salad to start please, and then I'll have the steak and kidney pie." Margaret ordered the fish. Gerry thought about warning her how bland it was, then reconsidered. She probably eats here all the time, she reasoned. Andrew ordered a burger and so did each of the boys. They sat back to wait.

Margaret eyed Gerry over her martini glass. "How are you enjoying The Maples?"

Gerry spoke slowly. "It's very nice. To be out of the city. It's the first time I've lived in the country." She grinned at Andrew. "But the neighbours are terrible."

Margaret quickly leaned forward. "Which ones? That Cathy?" Andrew laughed and Margaret sat up straight. "Oh, it was a joke. Ha ha."

David rolled his eyes. I thought only girls did that, Gerry mused. "Oh, Mum, lighten up." His mother shot him a vicious look. David quailed just as Doug strolled over. "Dad!" He looked happy to see his father.

"Hello, son. Boys." Doug kissed David and tousled the hair of the other two — or tried. He got Geoff but James pulled away.

"Excuse me." Margaret marched toward the ladies' room.

Doug sat down in her chair. "How are you, Andrew? Gerry?"

He didn't seem drunk. Andrew seemed friendly, so Gerry took her cue from him. "Great, Doug. You? We still on for tomorrow?"

"You bet. Wouldn't miss it."

As he rose, Andrew asked, "What's on tomorrow?"

Gerry smiled. "That's for us to know and you to find out — eventually."

Andrew subsided. "Oh."

As Margaret returned, Doug tipped an imaginary hat as they passed each other. Margaret snorted, her cheeks aflame. Thankfully, the food arrived, a welcome distraction. The burgers had different sauces and toppings and Andrew let Gerry try his: cheddar cheese and bacon. She admired James's more sophisticated palate — he'd chosen one topped with blue cheese and caramelized onions — and was surprised when she received only a scowl by way of reply. After that, she focused her attention on Andrew, and a bit on David, who seemed less resentful than the rest of his family.

After dessert — the Parsley specialized in cheesecake — Gerry had the salted caramel — came coffee. The two oldest boys made their excuses and left — a friend was picking them up to go to a party. Apparently the invitation didn't extend to David, and Gerry thought she saw tears of frustration shining in his eyes. His mother was deep in conversation with Andrew about the value of the figurines he'd inherited, and seemed not to notice David's discomfort.

Gerry leaned over. "Did you know Aunt Maggie well, David?"

David blinked, seeming to come back from a long way away. "Aunt Mags? Yeah, we went over there lots in the summer when we were little, to swim in the pool."

"What do you think of the cats?"

David smiled. "I loved the kittens. There was one named Bob — he's my favourite."

"Mine too! Though I don't let Marigold hear me say that. You should come over and see Bob sometime. And me. I'm sort of your aunt, too, or second cousin or something."

David shyly nodded but he looked pleased.

Gerry rose. "I shall leave you now, I think. Andrew, thank you so much. I enjoyed the meal. I must return the favour." Gerry felt herself assume that shark smile again. "Margaret, I feel I do know you a little better after tonight. David." And with quick kisses and a flick of her fingers, she made her exit.

"Whew." She stood in the hallway of the inn, was surprised to see Doug coming down the staircase that led to its rooms.

"I live here," he stated, "in exchange for my inestimable painting and gardening skills."

Gerry grinned. "You can't be drunk. You wouldn't be able to say 'inestimable.'"

He grinned back. "Believe it or not, it helps keeps me sober when I see how many people roll out of here drunk and then try to drive."

She saluted. "Only one glass of wine before supper, sir. Good to go. See you tomorrow."

He saluted back.

What a mystery, she thought, as she covered the short distance across gravel to her car. However did Margaret and Doug get together? The teenage attendant was long gone. "Oh," she said flatly. Somebody had keyed her car.

Gerry opened one eye then the other. Staying on her side, she looked out the window into a green pattern of gently rustling foliage. She felt unusually well this morning, considering she hadn't yet had her coffee. There was a small warmth curled up in the curve of her belly. She looked down, wondering who it would be, and was elated to see Marigold, soundly asleep. She must have left her door open when she went to bed. Then she groaned. The weekend. No Prudence. Time for the cat patrol.

She carefully climbed out of bed and got another surprise — Bob, asleep on her little black dress where she'd carelessly dropped it on the floor. He woke and stretched, his claws digging into the flimsy fabric. Gerry yelped and lunged. Bob dashed from the room, one claw still hooked in the cloth. "Argh!" Gerry picked up the dress halfway down the stairs and saw the snags. "Thanks, Bob. Now it's vintage."

She carried on down to the kitchen, Bob and Marigold following. As she passed through the dining room, the assembled company stretched and jumped down off their chairs. The boys and Stupid came in through the cat flap.

Gerry picked up Marigold and made a dash for the kitchen, closing the door on the mob. She fed the Princess first, got her coffee going, then prepared breakfast for everybody else and let them in. Grasping her mug, she opened the porch door and stepped out into the garden.

Another beautiful day. She stood and inhaled the clean air and watched a heron walk in slow motion from left to right, its gaze fixed on a point just a few inches ahead of its beak. Sailboats flirted with the lake breeze.

She walked down to the water's edge. To her left, the Ottawa flowed from the north. Hard to believe that in her father's time it had served to float softwood to Montreal from logging camps in northern Quebec and Ontario, and that it had been so polluted people had been afraid to swim in it.

To her right, she could see the ferry, in operation for nearly a hundred years between the little villages either side of the lake. The lake that is not a lake but part of a river.

She turned her back on the water to face the house. It graciously sprawled across the property. "Thank you, Auntie," she breathed. The crunch of a boat on the beach behind her made her swiftly turn.

"Weren't you expecting me?" Doug asked, throwing her a rope attached to the front of his canoe. She tied it to a ring through a post sunk in the ground for that purpose. "What's wrong?"

"Nothing. Much. Not while I live here."

"Wait till winter. No, really. Something's wrong."

Gerry sighed. "I have an enemy. Or maybe it was just kids." She stopped, stricken. "I didn't mean — "

He looked alert. "What?"

"Somebody keyed my car at the restaurant last night. A nice big X on the driver's door. Where I'll see it whenever I get in."

"Let's have a look."

The cats, having eaten, were beginning to stream outside. Marigold passed, on her way to her hydrangea. Bob and the boys zoomed by, full of nonsense. Stupid stalked off past the pool towards the neighbour's, while Mother sat Ronald down in front of her and gave him a thorough grooming. The rest of the honour guard, Blackie, Whitey, Mouse and Runt, watched gravely. Perhaps they'd all been similarly attended to by Mother in the past.

"Thirteen, fourteen, fifteen, sixteen, seventeen, eighteen, nineteen, twenty," Gerry counted. "That's everybody. I know twelve by name and I'm working on the other eight." She pointed at two enormous cats, one black with white spots, the other white with black spots. "I call them the cow cats. That's Harley and that's Kitty-Cat."

"Other way around," Doug commented, wryly.

"Drat!"

They examined the car.

"Well, you can either take it for bodywork or I can fix it for you."

"Do you have time?"

"It's a small job. Anyway, think about it. Today we have something else to do."

"Do you need me? 'Cause I have six cat boxes to clean out and a kitchen to tidy."

"I'll call if I need anything."

She left him to it. As she worked, she heard him whistling at his task. She went to her studio in the bamboo room, meaning to check something, looked up in amazement to find the morning gone.

Doug was still in the room that opened off the dining room. "Wow, you've got a lot done." They surveyed his work.

Now that the deep cases for her aunt's figurines were gone, the room was larger. Doug had removed its few bits of furniture, washed the walls and put up a picture rail on each wall. "I'll prime it this afternoon and paint tomorrow. Okay?"

"Okay. I've decided to have you repair the car."

"Good. Especially as it was probably one of my sons who did it. Or my wife." His tone was bitter.

Gerry kept silent. What could she say when she shared his suspicions? Everyone at their table had gotten up at some point to use the washroom. The two older boys had left early. She changed the subject. "Do you ever make art? I mean, I heard you're an artist."

He was about to speak when the phone rang.

"Excuse me." She ran to the kitchen. The phone was mounted on the wall and had a very long cord. Gerry pictured her aunt working there as she chatted with a friend.

"Gerry?" The voice was faint and frightened-sounding.

"Cathy?"

"Oh, Gerry, good. I'm at the hospital. Passing a stone, they tell me. Kidney." Cathy paused for breath. "Hurts. Charles. Can you?"

"Of course, of course. But a key?"

"I was in such a hurry when the ambulance came, I didn't lock up." She began to weep. "He'll be so hungry!"

"Shush, now. I'll go at once. And I'll come to see you."

She rushed over to Cathy's giant house, for once oblivious to its whimsical character. As she ran around the back to the kitchen door, Prince Charles's bass tones walloped her ears. "I'm coming, Charles, I'm coming!" she cried, as she almost fell through the door. Cathy hadn't said when she'd been taken to hospital. The poor dog must be frantic.

There was a scrabble of claws on hardwood as Charles got to his feet, tail wagging. He sat while Gerry patted him, then turned his gaze to the appropriate cupboard. Careful Cathy had stowed his kibble in a large mouse-proof garbage can. A scoop was dug into the kibble.

Gerry stood, perplexed, the massive bowl in one hand, scoop in the other. "Charles, how much?" She tried to quickly do mental math, estimating Charles's weight in cats, but her cats ate as much kibble as they wanted twice a day, so that didn't work. She sensed this method might not be appropriate for dogs, especially one as chunky as Charles.

One scoop went in the bowl. She looked at the still expectant dog. Another scoop, then. His bum stayed glued to the floor. "Another?" As the third scoop of food hit the bowl, Charles stood and began the odd noise — somewhere between a yelp and a bellow — that is the basset bark.

Gerry hastily put the bowl down, more to stop the noise than anything. As Charles ate, she threw more kibble into a bag, added a handful of dog biscuits from the basset-shaped crock on the counter, and the now slobbery, empty bowl.

Charles was taking great gulping laps of water, half of which he deposited on the floor, the other half on Gerry's feet. "Oh, nice, Charles. Thanks." She clipped on his leash.

For once Charles showed some energy. He dragged her to a shrub and lifted his leg. A steady stream doused the wretched plant. A few steps further on he located the cedar hedge, chose his spot with care, and backed into it. Gerry, unversed in the ways of dogs, watched in fascination as he pooped into the shrub.

"Wow, Charles, discreet or what?" She looked furtively around. No one to see. Cathy's own property. Surely there was no need to pick up this excellent hedge fertilizer, was there? She didn't have a bag, anyway. And Charles was already pulling her onward.

He peed on a large rock, a tree trunk and Cathy's gate. He peed on a telephone pole, a clump of weeds and a fire hydrant, then on The Maples' lamppost, a wooden half barrel of flowers, and finished up against the rear tire of Gerry's car. Then he flopped, exhausted.

Gerry coaxed him into the kitchen porch, where he sniffed the recycling bin and the garbage can, then dropped his nose and sniffed his way into the kitchen.

Marigold, waiting for lunch on the top of the fridge, flattened her ears and hissed. She tore away into the next room. Gerry still had Charles by the leash and hurriedly closed the kitchen door. What was she to do? Twenty cats and one basset hound. Quickly, she fixed herself a sandwich, another for Doug, and put Marigold's plate of meat atop the fridge.

Outside, she cast about for something to tie the dog up with. She remembered some clothesline she'd seen in the shed yesterday. Charles seemed happy as she tied him to the picnic table (associated with food, no doubt) on the back lawn and fetched him a bowl of water. He crawled under the table and went to sleep.

She found Marigold in a state of shock in the dining room with most of the others and scooped her up. "Okay, Princess, this is temporary." She placed the calico on the fridge and took the sandwiches to Doug.

"He okay?" Doug put down the roller and pulled a plastic bag over the paint tray. "Oh, thank you." He ate hungrily. "I've a thermos of tea there, if you want to share."

Gerry bit into her ham and cheese and asked, "Um, how long do you think kidney stones take to pass?"

Doug considered. "Not long, I think. Is that what she has? A few hours. If they don't pass, they might do surgery, I guess. I don't really know."

"How am I going to juggle twenty cats and the prince?"

"First of all, I would really like to see that. Secondly, I have every confidence in you. Why don't you visit Cathy this afternoon, check on her?"

"Yes, I said I would. Doesn't she have any family?"

"Well, she's local, but her family has kind of died out over the years. No kids that I know of. Go see her. I'll watch the prince."

Feeling overwhelmed, Gerry did a quick cat box clean, topped up the cat kibble, changed and drove to the hospital.

As always, the beautiful drive along the river road soothed her. Farms on one side, the vast expanse of the Ottawa, dotted with boaters enjoying their weekend, on the other. She counted five great blue herons spread out along the shore of the largest bay, standing, wading, each poised to strike. Then the river road ended, there was the quick rush of the highway, and soon she was struggling with the hospital parking system.

At reception she asked where Cathy might be. "When did she come in?" the woman asked.

"I'm not sure. Last night? Yesterday sometime?"

"She's probably still in emergency. Try there first."

Gerry pushed through swinging doors to emergency. It had been years since she'd been here. During one Christmas visit, when she was about ten, she'd fallen on the ice and cracked her wrist and been sent by the local doctor for an X-ray. She remembered leaning against her father for most of one day as they waited, her wrist aching, him gently distracting her with stories, candy, the newspaper comics.

She tried one office, was sent to another. Finally, she was allowed to enter emergency to look for her friend. She walked among the beds. Many people had a worried loved one at their side. An old woman was insulting a nurse. "You're no good. You're nervous. I can tell. Ouch! That hurt! Stop it!" The harassed nurse gave up on finding a vein and hurried away.

A blanketed lump faced the counter by which its gurney had been pushed. "Cathy?" Yes, but asleep. Gerry wandered around looking for a chair, finally dragged one from the waiting room. But Cathy wasn't where she'd left her.

"Gone for a scan," another nurse explained. "Won't be long."

Gerry plunked the chair where Cathy's bed had been. A woman sitting with an old man leaned forward. "Is she your relative?" It seemed easiest to nod. The woman continued. "Well, she's pretty doped up. She was here when we got here this morning. I think I heard the doctor say gall bladder."

"She told me kidney stone." A worried frown creased Gerry's forehead. The woman seemed affronted.

"Well, I'm only telling you what I heard!"

She looked tired, so Gerry thanked her and enquired about her husband. Unexpectedly, he opened his eyes and spoke. "I'm still here, you know!"

At this point, thankfully, Cathy reappeared and was parked. She was awake but her eyes were dopey-looking. "She was afraid, she told me, she was afraid…the canoe shouldn't have been there… the boys, the boys…she was afraid…I'm sorry, Maggie." Her gaze cleared. "I'm sorry. I'm babbling. Surgery, they say. Charles?"

"At my place with Doug."

"Oh, Doug. Such a sweet little boy. Tell Charles…tell Charles…"

"I'll give him your love," Gerry murmured as Cathy fell asleep.

PART 2

TEACUPS

*S*he waited in the dining room for the man to finish painting. The smell was unpleasant, but she was hungry.

She liked men. She dozed, remembering her first owner. She'd put out a paw through the slats of the cage at the pet store and he'd clasped it gently. When he took her out of the cage she'd gone limp, moulding herself to his chest. And when he'd begun looking at another, more playful kitten in the cage, she'd put out her paw again, this time to bat one of her brothers in the face. The man had laughed and said, "She's made her selection."

She'd grown up in his apartment, never going outside except when he'd bundle her into the cat carrier for a trip to the vet.

Sometimes his little children would visit, but mostly it had been her and him, alone together.

Then one morning she'd woken to find the bed empty, the man swinging like a catnip mouse on a string, swinging high from a rope and the hall light fixture. There was the same bad smell as when the woman had died in her bed, a similar absence. She'd crouched, waiting.

She never saw the children again, but a woman who smelled like them came after a few days and took her away, left her at the vet.

So when another woman had selected her from a few adult cats in the cage at the vet's, First Cat wasn't surprised. She hadn't even had to put out her paw; they'd looked at each other and she felt the woman knew.

The painting man came out of the room and closed the door. He took in the room full of cats. "Well, well, let's see what we can do."

He seemed to know she was special, put the right food in the right spot, fed the others. "Oh my God! Prince Charles!" He clutched his head and ran out the door.

She could hear him praising the dog. Apparently, it was still alive. She stretched and hopped down from fridge to counter to floor.

The others made way as she passed. "Small but mighty," she recalled the woman, the old woman, saying proudly.

Outside, and from under the hydrangea, she watched as the man fetched water for the dog, heard its sloppy drinking.

It subsided back under the picnic table. The man had just lit a cigarette and sat at the table looking at the lake when the phone rang. He cursed and went inside.

She crept up on the dog. It lay on its side, twitching and moaning. It smelt like — dog. She passed it and made for the shore. The man had pulled his canoe high up out of the water, presumably so it wouldn't bump against the rocks. She sniffed one end of the rope; the woman — the young woman — had touched it. She followed the rope with her nose, hopped up on the prow of the canoe, smelt the man who'd just fed her. And in between?

She dropped into the canoe, stepped delicately around damp patches, found the man's jacket, curled up and slept.

She woke when she heard the young woman's car pull in and the dog begin its absurd barking. She yawned and stretched and wandered over to Yalta.

She'd never understood why the old woman and her friends laughed when speaking of the place, or why the laughter increased when the boys, known to the woman as Winston, Franklin and Joseph, made their appearance on their chosen hunting ground around the pool.

The woman would say, "It just all came together and Yalta it became." And the guests would laugh knowingly.

A human thing, it must be, but First Cat didn't even understand cat jokes, such as the ones played by Second Cat, the boys and certain of the others. Such as the one being played even now. She crouched behind a screen of ivy and watched.

Defiance was asleep, stretched out on his side as had been the dog. Very slowly, Second Cat was creeping up on him, and equally slowly, the boys were doing likewise, surrounding him.

First Cat backed away. She knew the scene was soon to erupt. Sure enough, she'd gone only a few steps towards some flowering plants, green freckled bells clustered along upright stalks, when all hell broke loose.

Either Defiance had awoken or the others had pounced—the result was the same—a rolling spitting ball of angry cat fur. After a brief look, First Cat continued her walk through the formal garden, past the green dangling bells, some large plants with big white trumpets for flowers, and some violet-blue flowers ranged on tall spikes. By these latter plants she paused. She smelled something, something she remembered.

Second Cat zoomed by, then Defiance, then the boys. They disappeared through the hedge into the neighbour's yard, where First Cat never went. She was hungry again, and tired, and went inside.

5

Gerry spent the next few days between cat and dog maintenance, hospital visiting and supervising Doug finishing what they now called the gallery. Cathy had surgery late Monday, and by Wednesday noon was able to be brought home.

Prince Charles was already in residence, and Gerry left the two happily dozing on the sofa, promising to come by that evening to check on them.

"Whew!" she remarked to Prudence when she returned home. "That was intense!"

Prudence was having her afternoon break on the screened back porch and Gerry joined her with a coffee and a sigh. "Ah," she said as she leaned back.

A perfect late June day. Bees buzzed in the garden, butterflies and dragonflies danced near the shore. A light breeze rustled through the Virginia creeper that partly covered the porch. A squirrel chittered high in a tree. A plane hummed overhead.

A few cats were going about their business. Most of them slept in the daytime, but from time to time one wandered by. Marigold sat on a chair near the women. Bob and Stupid faced each other on the path to Yalta, about ten feet apart, both sitting in the sphinx position, only their tail tips twitching.

"Who'll win, do you suppose?" asked Gerry.

"Oh, Bob, of course. He's the good guy. Don't they always win?"

"In a perfect world." Gerry paused. "Thank you for putting in the extra time, Prudence. Things got kind of crazy, what with the dog sleeping on the porch, the cats upset by him and my work deadline."

"I think you did very well by Cathy," said Prudence slowly. "You take after your aunt. She was kind too."

Gerry was embarrassed. "Oh, well, I know she's alone and I like her. And anyway, isn't everyone in this village sort of related? We most of us come from the same place. Devon, wasn't it?"

Prudence nodded. "There was a village of Lovering in Devon and when they started coming here in the 1800s, they made another one. All the Coneybears and Petherbridges, Parsleys, Muxworthys, Catfords, Striblings."

"And Cricks," said Gerry, referring to Prudence's family.

"Yes, the Cricks as well, though I was a Catford before I married."

"Like my Gramma Ellie!" Gerry exclaimed. "See? We're related too. Are you on the family tree?"

Prudence smiled faintly. "I suppose I must be."

Bob and Stupid were now about five feet apart. "Right," said Gerry. "I'm going for a swim." She marched over to the two cats and stood between them. "You two should be friends." She picked up Bob and went closer to Stupid. "Stupid, wouldn't you like to be friends with Bob?" Stupid turned and walked away as Bob struggled in Gerry's arms.

She continued down to Yalta, took off her clothes and walked down the steps, entering the water with a shudder of pleasure. Bob sat on her shirt and groomed, embarrassed at having his standoff interrupted.

She floated on her back, contemplating the patches of blue visible through the surrounding trees' leaves. She'd gotten in the habit of skinny-dipping recently. The pool was surrounded by an ivy-covered chain-link fence and no one should be on the property unless she knew about it. Besides, who would drop in on her? She hadn't made a lot of friends. Yet.

And was she related to a lot of the locals? She walked up the stairs, towelled off and basked on a lounge chair. Bob sat nearby companionably. Really, she thought, he and Marigold would be enough. And Mother was sweet. And you couldn't have Mother without Ronald, she supposed, and the honour guard. Oh, they all had their good points. Except Stupid and Lightning. Stupid spent half his time on the neighbour's property. Who was the neighbour? Weren't they sick of Stupid coming over into their garden all the time?

She dressed and went to the gate in the cedar hedge that separated the two properties. The families must have been close once, to have a gate installed. "Hello?" she called cautiously. "Stupid?" She opened the gate, suddenly worried about trespassing.

"Hello," a quavery voice replied. "Come through. Is it Gerry, my dear Maggie's niece?"

Gerry called "Yes" as she passed along a narrow path overgrown by balsam.

The voice continued, "A little further. You're almost there. Hello."

She'd stepped out onto a patch of soggy, ragged lawn. Further up, near the house, an elderly man sat in a chair in a gazebo. A grey cat sat on his lap. The man waved a hand, gesturing for her to approach.

The house, a Victorian monstrosity, loomed darkly behind him, its turrets and gables, widow's walk and gingerbread house trim all clashing horribly. Gerry thought it was wonderful, itched for her sketch pad.

She squelched through the wet grass to the dryer ground where the gazebo stood, remarking cheerfully, "My feet are wet."

"It floods in springtime. It's much lower than your property." He stuck out a hand. "I'm Blaise. Blaise Parminter. And this is Graymalkin."

Gerry took the hand gingerly, avoiding putting her own anywhere near the cat. "That, sir, is Stupid."

Blaise covered the cat's ears loosely. "Shush, now. How would you like to be called Stupid every day? I could never understand why a kind person like Maggie would call him that. Of course he just got meaner." He added softly, "He's my friend."

"I can see that. Do you feed him?"

"Only human food: salmon, tuna, chicken."

"Yet he keeps returning to my place. I wonder why?"

"Well, he needs the company of the other cats, I suppose."

"You have my permission to try to keep him with you at night if you like."

"I would like that." He spoke directly to the cat. "Will you sleep at my house tonight, Graymalkin?" The response was a purr. Stupid looked at Gerry, as if to say, "See what you missed out on? Who's stupid now?"

Gerry said goodbye and walked thoughtfully home. Prudence was feeding the teeming throng. "One less plate, Prudence. Stupid is going to live next door with Mr. Parminter."

Prudence nodded. "He always did like that cat. Said he was misunderstood. And Stupid never scratched or bit him."

"Were he and Aunt Maggie 'friends'?"

"Oh, not like that. But real friends who cared about each other. They liked the same music, poetry. Mr. Parminter is a poet, you know. Quite well respected. Helped start the literary festival."

"Lovering has a literary festival?"

"Yes, and two art societies. Culture goes on outside of cities too."

"I know it does." They'd finished washing the cat plates and Prudence was washing the floor. "I'm just going to the graveyard, Prudence. I'll see you Friday."

Gerry picked a few flowers, then walked the short distance to the little church. Lovering, for such a small town, was denominationally well represented with five churches. A few minutes' walk away was St. Anne's Anglican Church, a small stone chapel built by landowners in the mid-1800s. It had a simple flat steeple for its single small bell and a little churchyard between the church and a few apple trees.

Gerry walked to the back of the churchyard where the memorial wall was. She remembered her father telling her that behind the church had been a pig farm, and that the highlight of his Sundays had been being allowed to run around the back of the church after service, to hang on the farmyard gate and watch the pigs.

The farm was no longer there, though the farmhouse, gate and field were, beyond the barbed wire fence that marked the end of the churchyard. The memorial wall was a recent addition, built when the space for graves and their bulky markers grew scarce. Here were attached brass plaques for some of Gerry's family — her parents, her Aunt Maggie. Others, like her grandparents, had their names chiselled in black or grey granite stones where their ancestors' names had preceded them.

She paused and touched first her mother's, then her father's, then Aunt Maggie's plaques, and laid a few blooms on each, then sighed. She still had to look in on Cathy.

She found her friend up and cooking. "You shouldn't be doing that!" she admonished, taking the frying pan away and sitting her down.

"Just eggs and toast," Cathy protested weakly. "Add a couple more and eat with us." Gerry scrambled the eggs, toasted bread and made a pot of tea. "It's so good to be home," Cathy stated. "You have no idea."

"No, I don't. I've never stayed overnight in hospital."

"I have a great admiration for the nurses. They work so hard. As do the doctors, I'm sure, though you don't see as many of them. But the noises and the voices. Especially at night. People get weird and cranky. I'm exhausted."

"Then you must have an early night." Gerry put down her cutlery. "Cathy, when you were dopey the first day, you said Aunt Maggie was afraid. Actually you said 'she' but I thought it was Aunt Maggie because then you said, 'I'm sorry, Maggie.' And something about the canoe being in the wrong place and the boys."

"Did I, dear? I don't remember."

"Don't remember saying it or don't remember Aunt Maggie being afraid?"

Cathy looked blank. "Neither, I'm afraid. But I'll think on it, Gerry, I really will." She reached down and petted Charles's head. "Thank you for caring for Charles. He seems fine."

"Prudence and Doug helped. Charles is an easy dog. I quite like him. Makes a change from the cats. Oh, I almost forgot. I have something for you." She fetched a large tote bag and took out a flat paper parcel tied with string.

Cathy handled the object before unwrapping it. "Well, I guess it's a painting or something." She surveyed the neatly framed drawing. "Why, it's my house! It's Fieldcrest! Oh, it's funny! It looks like a lady. Thank you, Gerry."

"It's part of a series of portraits of local houses I'm working on. But yours was the first, the one that inspired me. I may ask to borrow it back, okay? If I give a show, which I'm planning to do."

"A show? Where?"

"I thought at the house in a few rooms on the ground floor. With nibbles and wine, of course, to pull people in."

"Oh, would you like me to do the nibbles? Little cheesy tarts and so on?"

"That would be wonderful, Cathy. I was hoping you would. But you should rest now." Charles and Cathy slowly accompanied Gerry along the hall from kitchen to front door, where the women said their goodnights.

6

The next few weeks passed quickly as Gerry settled into the summer routine of The Maples.

Up around seven, feed cats, do cat boxes, drink coffee on porch staring at lake. Work. She was still receiving some work through her Toronto connections, but not much, and, worried she'd experience a drop in income, put an ad in the local paper, offering to immortalize people's children, pets, houses, gardens. So far, she'd received one commission: to paint the garden of a local amateur gardener, famous (so Prudence told her) for her peonies and roses.

After work, lunch, then, if she had no appointments, more work. Some days she saw no one; others, only Prudence. She saw Andrew across the road going to and coming from work, or working in his garden, but only to wave to or briefly chat with. Since the uncomfortable dinner at the Parsley, he'd kept his distance.

The cat feeding and cat boxes were repeated at four, and around five every day, Gerry usually poured herself a cold glass of rosé and thought about supper while soaking in the pool or sitting on the porch. Evenings she spent on the porch, cheating the mosquitoes, reading or sketching as the summer light held until almost ten.

It was on one such evening around eight that she heard a car arrive at the front of the house. She went through and peered out one of the windows through its flimsy curtain. Her aunt's lawyer, Cecil Muxworthy, was getting out of his car. Never a good thing,

Gerry thought, to see a lawyer at the door, then reprimanded herself. He might be here to give her news of another legacy! She opened the door. "Hi, Cece, how are you?"

"Fine, Gerry, fine. You got a moment? Something's come up."

She got him a cup of tea and they sat on the porch.

"God, it's lovely here."

"Where do you live, Cece?"

"Oh, in the village, in one of those condos next to the United church."

Surprised he couldn't afford better — the condos were narrow townhouses with tiny gardens, suitable for the elderly, and Cece couldn't be much more than fifty — Gerry mumbled, "Oh, those are nice and convenient for shopping. You don't need the car."

"Yes. Convenient. I use the living room as my office." He seemed nervous. "Look, Gerry, there's been a complaint about one of the cats." He looked guilty. "It's my fault. I happened to visit Mr. Parminter — he's one of my clients — and he mentioned you'd given him one of the cats."

"I did. The cat was unhappy here and I thought Mr. Parminter seemed lonely."

"Well, I appreciate that, but I mentioned it to my wife and she said something about how nice it was of you to Margaret, and now Margaret is saying you've broken one of the main conditions of the will — that you keep the cats."

"Oh, for heaven's sake! How old is Mr. Parminter? Ninety-something? How long can he live? Just say the cat's a loan and that I'll take care of it again when Mr. Parminter is no longer able. Good enough?"

The lawyer looked relieved. "Yes, I think that could work. I'm sorry about that, but your cousin…"

Gerry finished his sentence. "My cousin wishes I would go away and she could live here or sell up and have the money. I don't blame her. I've been very lucky. And she's being petty. Is there anything else?" She sounded exasperated.

He got up to go. "Thank you for the tea. My wife and I wondered if you'd like to come for dinner some time. Perhaps this weekend?"

Gerry softened. "Oh, that would be nice. Thank you."

He nodded. "My wife will call you. Good night."

"Good night." Gerry stood at the front door and waved him away. She closed the door and sat on the front step, screened by the shrubs that separated the little half-circle of driveway from the road.

Left over from the days when the carriage would pull up to the front door for the ladies to get out, she mused. So gracious. And the side entrance for the men after they'd put away the horses. The old shed/garage must have once been the stable. That reminded her of her car door, expertly sanded and the paint colour matched by Doug.

Across the street she saw Andrew moving in his lit-up living room. He bent down and disappeared. Then he appeared to stretch toward the ceiling. Is he exercising? No, he's dusting! she realized. He's dusting his china. I wonder if he finds it soothing.

The light went out in the room and she suddenly felt embarrassed, as though she'd been snooping. Bob strolled up and she stroked his head. "Time for bed, little man?" He yawned and she copied him. "Time for bed."

Prudence came the next morning, so after breakfast, Gerry thankfully left the cat dishes and boxes to her, and drove to view the garden she was to paint. It took her about fifteen minutes to drive from her southern end of Lovering, through the village proper, and from there, west to the well-established development where her future client lived.

After a few wrong turns and frequently consulting a local map she kept in the glove compartment, she found the address and parked, studied the house and its front garden.

The house was square and so was the garden. The house was white shingled with pink trim and a pale blue door upon which a heart-shaped wreath of ivy was hung. The garden was similar: no lawn, but filled with roses, peonies and other assorted blooms in white and pink with a touch of blue. Hmm, thought Gerry, very chocolate box, but nice.

"Hello!"

Gerry jumped. The voice was that of a pleasant-looking man — plump, middle-aged, spectacled — who was walking a tiny white dog. "Are you the artist my wife was telling me about?"

Gerry got out of the car. "Yes, I'm Gerry Coneybear. How do you do?"

"I'm Al Shipton and I'm pleased to meet you. What do you think of the garden?"

"It's very sweet, Mr. Shipton, and beautifully complements the house. Your wife's work?"

His eyes twinkled. "She designs. I do the heavy lifting. Come on. She's excited. This painting is a birthday present for her." He picked the dog up. "And this is Mitzi."

Mrs. Shipton was in the kitchen. She'd prepared a tray of pastries and coffee and brought it into the living room. She was Mr. Shipton's female counterpart except she wore contact lenses instead of spectacles. Gerry showed her samples of her work and, predictably, Mrs. Shipton picked a conservative style. The house was to be included in the painting. As she left, Gerry concluded she was a nice woman but with little sense of humour. When she'd seen the original sketch Gerry had done of Cathy's house — the house as a blousy matron in floppy hat and full skirt — she'd passed right over it.

Never mind, thought Gerry, as she took some photos of the property; at five hundred a pop, a few more of these commissions would be most welcome. She'd left Mrs. Shipton a few of her cards with a request she give them to her gardening friends.

She grabbed a quick lunch at the donut shop by the highway on-ramp and went home. Prudence handed her a message. "Mrs. Muxworthy called and asked if Saturday night was okay. Here's her number." When Gerry called, the phone went to an answering machine so she just confirmed and hung up.

That afternoon she drafted a rough idea for the Shipton painting. The birthday was in three weeks and she wanted to work while the impression was still fresh in her mind. But first, to relieve her feelings, she quickly sketched the house, first as a wedding cake with plants as decorations, then as a chocolate box, with large gooey confections spilling out of windows and into the garden.

During a coffee break, she went into the gallery. It was now painted a dull off-white, and rows of tiny lights had been installed near the ceiling. She'd also had Doug give a coat of dove-grey to the wide-planked flooring. The room was ready. Now, where was the art?

One wall was going to be for large posters from her *Mug the Bug* comic strip. One wall would be for her series of humorous house portraits. She'd almost finished the one of Mr. Parminter's house, its varied architectural features flying off in all directions. She had ideas for the other two walls, just not yet acted upon.

Back in the dining room, she walked from chair to chair, patting each occupant and explaining her plan. "Just for one or two days, guys, you'll all have to go either outside or upstairs. I'm going to need this room for the reception, okay?"

Eyes, green or yellow, blinked lazily. Some purrs could be heard, a few of the reclining forms sat up and stretched. A thought occurred to her and she went to find Prudence. "Prudence, did my aunt ever appear frightened of anyone or anything?"

Prudence put down the mop she was wielding and considered. "Not frightened, exactly. But there were a few times I found her holding a letter and just staring, looking worried. When I asked her if anything was wrong, she said it was just bills. Why?"

"Cathy said something, very general, nothing in particular, about Aunt Maggie being afraid. It was probably just bills. Which reminds me, have you noticed a smell over where the weeping field is?"

Prudence nodded. "Maggie was meaning to replace it with a tank but never got around to it."

"Mm. I better get that done." She wandered to her studio, thinking, there goes a chunk of the money Maggie left me for the house.

That night, she sat in her aunt's office in one of the little rooms formerly for servants. Gerry had put off sorting her aunt's papers, feeling it an invasion of privacy, but now it seemed necessary. She needed to understand what work had recently been done on the house and what bills she might expect in the future.

Marigold kept her company, inevitably sitting on the very pile of papers Gerry needed. She picked the little creature up and cuddled her. "You've gained a little weight, haven't you, Princess?" Gerry put her on a pillow she suspected her aunt had kept on the desk for that purpose. But Marigold simply sat on a different pile of papers. When Gerry got to those, she put the cat on the pillow again and this time she stayed there.

Gerry had cleared the desk and now dived into the small black filing cabinet. "I should be methodical," she muttered, but groaned when she saw the first file was marked BILLS — Miscellaneous. It bulged. The one after it, slightly thinner, was CATS. "You guys are important too," she said to Marigold and removed the file.

Each cat had one or two sheets of paper describing how they looked, acted; where Maggie had gotten them; all their trips to the vet. "Holy cow!" Gerry exclaimed when she pulled out the VET file and estimated the yearly bill. She'd certainly need a few commissions to cover that!

All method now lost, she began pulling out only the files that interested her. There was another exclamation when she saw the amounts, year after year, for property taxes. "Well, Marigold, this has been a wake-up call. I need to figure the yearly outgoings and then calculate how much I'll need to earn."

She was feeling a bit daunted so went back to the beginning of the filing cabinet. "Knowledge is power," she told the little cat. "It's not knowing that can wreck things."

She worked until she got up to 'H' for HYDRO, then went to bed, dreaming of giant pink and white numbers chasing her through Mrs. Shipton's garden.

Thunder boomed and lightning cracked the night, and she had trouble getting back to sleep. She finally got out of a restless bed early and faced a rainy day. She performed the routine for the cats but felt stale, and decided to take an umbrella and explore Lovering properly. A short drive brought her to the edge of town where commercial activity began.

"Ah, coffee." She poked around in the tiny gift shop–café, then walked to the next shop that interested her — full of fabrics. It was such a pleasure to handle the differently patterned tablecloths, napkins, aprons and placemats. They had clothes too. She bought a black fedora with a red feather jauntily stuck on one side and segued to the next store — a patisserie — where she bought a quiche, a small one, for her supper, and an almond croissant to consume immediately.

She was sitting feeling very pleased with her rainy-day activity and thinking, "When pressed for money, go shopping!" when Doug came in, bought coffee and a ham and cheese roll and plunked himself next to her.

"What's up, boss?" he enquired pleasantly.

"I've escaped."

"We all need to do that from time to time." Melted cheese oozed out of his sandwich and Gerry found herself salivating.

"Looks good."

"So order one." She did and felt really decadent, having eaten her dessert first.

"Doug, did my aunt ever appear frightened about anything? More than worried, frightened?"

Doug wiped his mouth and looked grave. "She wanted me to keep it quiet but I guess now she's gone...she asked me to keep on the look-out for signs someone might try to hurt the cats — spot traps or poisoned meat. I never found anything."

Gerry didn't know why but she felt a bit disappointed. "But nothing directed against her, personally?"

"Not that I knew of. Gotta go."

Gerry finished her sandwich and, the urge to shop slaked by her mini-spree, went home for a rainy-day nap. That evening, working late again, she finished the painting of the Shipton house.

She hoped it would be okay with the Shiptons; she'd put Mitzi sitting in one of the windows. If they didn't like it, she could always paint the little dog out.

She yawned and went around the house, checking doors and windows, had a last scrape at the cat boxes, said goodnight to the cats, who were mostly all inside, counted them, as she'd formed a habit of doing, and found four short. Bob and the boys, of course. Probably outside, stalking damp mice.

She looked out onto the sloping back lawn. Rain was still falling and a mist rose from the water's surface. She was looking for cats but instead saw a canoe cross from right to left, pause while its occupant looked at her house, then continue on its way upriver.

Who would be out after midnight in such weather and why were they looking at her home?

She shivered and broke her fearful mood. Nonsense! Whoever it was, they were probably looking at all the houses along the shore, just enjoying the summer night. But, her sensible self continued, in the rain?

As she settled to sleep, she was thankful for the calm presence of Marigold at her side and, a little later, a wet Bob, who leapt onto her bed, groomed himself dry, then curled at her feet. Her last thought before sleep reclaimed her was that she resembled the effigy of a medieval lady she'd seen on a tomb, her companion animal likewise disposed.

Prudence arrived earlier than usual the next morning, to be met by a groggy Gerry. "You look a bit rough," the housekeeper remarked, setting out the cat dishes. "Better make your coffee."

"Thanks, I will." Prudence opened the kitchen door and, as the hairy mass exploded into the room, the women took their coffee into the winter living room next door. A bird flew into the window they were facing and Gerry let out a small scream.

"Whoa, who's a bit jumpy?"

"Not a lot of sleep. Did the household expenses, actually, two nights ago, and I'm a bit discouraged. How will I be able to pay for this place? And the vet bills!"

"Have you thought about giving art lessons? Private or classes? There was a guy who used to do that but he moved away. A lot of retirees studied with him."

"I never taught before," Gerry said slowly.

"It's almost August. Design yourself a nice little ad and put it in the local paper. You could teach here."

"You think?"

"Yeah. And make them supply their own materials. You don't want to buy that stuff and then have nobody show up."

"Well, we'd start with sketching, anyway, so just paper and pencils would be needed. It might be fun. Good idea, Prudence. What would I do without you?"

A pleased-looking Prudence smiled into her coffee. "It's all part of the service."

Gerry drew the ad and drove to the office of the *Lovering Herald*, located in a cute little house in the village. "Run it for two or three weeks, end of August, early September, alongside the ads for music and dance lessons," said the genial proprietor, who, with his young daughter, seemed to be operating the business alone.

"Um, I'm going to have an art show at my home, maybe in September. Could you run an ad for that too?"

"Sure could. And we'll come and cover it. Give you a nice write-up in the paper. Won't we, Judith?"

The girl, tall and dark, nodded shyly. Her father continued, "She likes art, Judy does. Took it in high school. Maybe she'll take one of these courses of yours, eh, Jude?"

Gerry smiled at the girl. "That would be nice, Mr., er — "

"Parsley. Bill. And my daughter, Judith."

More Parsleys, thought Gerry, getting into her car. I've really got to study that family tree, see who I'm related to.

After her bad night, she napped again that afternoon, woke up as Prudence was leaving. She yawned. "I'm all turned around. You're leaving early."

"That's why I came early. It's my day for a visit with Mother."

"Where does your mother live, Prudence?"

"She doesn't live anywhere. She's buried not far from your parents at St. Anne's."

Gerry spoke slowly. "So, you're going to the graveyard?"

Prudence also spoke slowly, choosing her words with care. "No. I'm going to see Mrs. Smith, a medium. Mother speaks to me through her."

"I see."

"No, you don't, and you think I'm foolish, but I believe in it and it does me good." Prudence said all this in such matter-of-fact tones that Gerry had nothing more to say except, "Well, then, enjoy yourself."

And Prudence marched down the road, pushing the empty baby carriage.

On her way to the Muxworthys for dinner, Gerry picked up a bottle of her favourite rosé. She parked in the church lot, as Cece had instructed her, and walked to number 3.

The small front yard had a paved path right up to the door and a little bed of hollyhocks, cherry tomatoes and herbs. It was charming, and she told Cece so when he opened the door. "It's Bea's work. Come and meet her."

A large woman came to greet them. "I'm Bea. Nice to meet you, Gerry."

Gerry handed her the wine and Bea spun her wheelchair around, saying, "I'll put it in the freezer. That'll cool it quick."

The small room was sparsely furnished. An easy chair and chaise longue faced the TV, while along one wall were ranged Cece's desk, filing cabinets and a table with stacks of files. "Come through," Bea called.

The living room opened into a kitchen with table and chairs and another sitting area beyond: a glass conservatory with pots of flowering plants. Beyond that, Gerry could see Cece's car.

"It's MS," Bea was saying. "Some days I can walk and some I can't. Today I can't." She put on oven mitts and opened the oven door. "It's ratatouille. They have such wonderful vegetables at the farmer's market each week. And it's just across the way."

Gerry, who'd been vaguely aware such a market existed, mumbled something about not being much of a cook.

"Neither am I, really, but there's such good produce in the summer, I'm inspired. Believe me, by January, I'm reheating store-bought meat pie and opening cans of soup. Cece, get out the cheese and paté and I'll slice the bread. Oh, and the wine. That's everything."

Cece poured the wine and Bea raised her glass. "Bon appétit!" she said in a passable imitation of Julia Child. Caught off guard, Gerry laughed. "Oh, good," Bea sighed. "Now I can relax. You wouldn't believe how uptight some people get around a wheelchair."

"Well, I was a little," Gerry admitted, helping herself to the ratatouille. "This is delicious."

"Dip your bread in the sauce," Cece encouraged, demonstrating.

"This paté is pretty good, too," said Gerry, spreading it on the bread.

"Farmer's market," said Bea. "Top me up, darling." She held her glass out to Cece. The look he gave her made Gerry suddenly aware of how long it had been since someone had looked at her like that. Lucky Bea. Lucky Cece.

After supper Bea showed Gerry her collection of orchids. "More will be in bloom in the winter. I don't know why. Stress?"

Gerry took some photos of the orchids that were in bloom. One in particular — a pansy orchid with white-edged and splotched maroon petals — attracted her. Perhaps she could do individual plant portraits, miniatures maybe, and sell them in a local gift shop.

Suddenly, she felt a burst of optimism. She would make it work, earn enough money to support The Maples, the cats, and enjoy herself at the same time. "Thank you so much," she said, impulsively bending to embrace Bea. "You've cheered me up."

That night, filled with a renewed sense of purpose, she tackled the bottom drawer of her aunt's filing cabinet. There, underneath the hanging file folders and pushed into the back, she found the letters.

7

August passed in a whirl of deadlines, visits with prospective clients, and telephone conversations fielding questions about her upcoming classes.

Word had spread even before the ads appeared in the *Herald*, and she had a few interested people.

The Shiptons were thrilled with the painting of their house, and Gerry was invited to toast it hanging over the fireplace in their living room. Far from objecting to Mitzi at the window, they ordered another painting — with Mitzi as the main subject. Gerry took some photographs of the dog inside and in the garden, and was relieved when Mrs. Shipton gave her until Christmas. "It's my gift from Al, so you have until December twenty-fourth."

The first classes would start after Labour Day, and, after consulting with the students, the time was settled for Wednesdays from one to four. This was a Prudence day, so Gerry could count on her to tidy in the morning, care for the cats, and prepare tea and snacks for the mid-afternoon break.

After some thought, she decided she'd teach in the bamboo room/studio. First, it was charming and the students would be impressed and interested to view part of the house's art collection on its walls. Second, it was away from the cats and only Marigold came in there, so, hopefully, if anyone had a cat allergy, it would be a safe place for them. And third, all of Gerry's art supplies, easel and drawing table were there, handy if she needed to demonstrate.

She and Prudence moved the furniture around, put some of it in the big foyer next door. "They can drop their coats in here," Gerry said, "then come through."

"Maggie used to close off this room after Christmas. Too difficult to heat. Poorly insulated."

"Well, if this room's too cold, we'll just have to move to the winter living room next to the kitchen and make a nice fire. That is, assuming anyone wants to continue after Christmas."

"Some local businesses close in January and February. It's so cold and a lot of people stay in or just struggle out for work and grocery shopping."

"Is it as bad as that?"

Prudence grimly nodded. "You should get your firewood in now. We have to stack it in the garage and bring it into the house as we need it."

"But it's August," wailed Gerry. "Can't we still enjoy summer?"

Prudence was relentless. "Yes, but you need to get the chimneys swept and the oil furnace serviced. Oh, and top up the oil tank."

"My God, you mean I have three types of heating? Oil, wood and electric baseboards?"

"Yes, and you'll need all of them by January. You ain't in Toronto anymore."

"Anything else?" Gerry added sweetly.

"Did you want me to call the Hudsons about the septic again?"

The Hudsons were the only local contractor who seemed available to work on the house's odour problem, and they'd postponed twice. Gerry's voice took on an absent-minded tone. "Yes, please, Prudence. Just don't let them start on a Wednesday! Unless they make it before Labour Day, which is beginning to look doubtful."

She surveyed the portraits, some done in charcoal, some in coloured crayon or chalk, which adorned the walls of the bamboo room. "Who drew these?"

Prudence seemed surprised. "Why, I thought you knew. Your aunt did."

"Why didn't she sign them?"

"She did. But on the back."

Gerry took one down — a portrait of a thin elderly woman with forbidding lips — and reversed it. There, neatly printed on the paper that her aunt must have glued to the frame, were the words, 'Eliz. Coneybear, by Marg. Coneybear, her granddaughter,' followed by Aunt Maggie's signature.

"So all the drawings in this style are Aunt Maggie's?"

Prudence nodded.

"Fantastic. I'm putting them in the show. They'll be the third wall and there are enough of them to spill over into the foyer. Let's do a count — I seem to remember there are some in her bedroom — and then have a coffee."

It was a fascinating ancestral treasure hunt. As Prudence and Gerry went from room to room, turning portraits over, Gerry discovered a great-aunt or -uncle, cousins from two centuries before. Aunt Maggie had always noted the subject's relationship to her, so it was easy enough for Gerry to extrapolate their relationship to her. "Look, Prudence, a Crick."

Prudence smiled thinly. "Yes, he has the look of my husband." There was a lack of enthusiasm in her voice that warned Gerry away from the subject. They took their break on the back porch. A light rain was beginning.

"I'll be sorry when it's too cold to sit here," Gerry began, leaning back in her chair and putting her clasped hands behind her head. A small drop of water fell on her nose. "That's funny," she said, sitting upright. Another larger drop fell in her coffee.

Prudence got up and went into the house, returning with two umbrellas. The women sat glumly and drank their coffee. "Who do I call for roofs?" Gerry asked grimly.

"It'll make a good story to tell your children." Prudence's lips were twitching. Gerry couldn't help it. She laughed.

She laughed again that Friday afternoon when Bea, having walked with the aid of a stick from her house to the farmer's market, held up a suggestively shaped tripartite carrot and raised her eyebrows.

"Yes," said Gerry, "but chopped up in a stew."

"Ouch," said the nice young man selling the carrots. They also bought onions and potatoes for the stew, and late raspberries to eat with ice cream, then went back to Bea's house and started cooking.

"How's the show coming?" asked Bea, pouring them each a glass of red wine.

"Oh, I meant to ask you. Do you think the third weekend in September would be good?"

"Let me think." She looked at the calendar on the side of the fridge. "Film society, music club, historical society, literary festival. Nope. Third weekend works fine."

"Do you really participate in all that?" Gerry asked, awe in her voice.

"Church choir, cooking for Meals on Wheels, baking squares for funeral receptions." Bea finished checking her activities off on her fingers. "Oh, and helping Cece if he needs me."

"Wow." Gerry handed Bea the chopped onions. "I think I'm going to cry."

"Don't feel bad. Remember, I'm a kept woman." She waggled her hips and lurched against the stove. "Damn. Time to sit down."

Gerry took over, under Bea's supervision, and by the time Cece walked in there was garlic bread, a crisp salad, and a beef stew, redolent of fresh thyme from Bea's garden.

"Cheers!" said Gerry. "To the weekend."

"To the weekend!" chimed the others.

She wilted. "Actually, I don't even know what a weekend is supposed to feel like anymore. When you work for yourself you just seem to keep pushing every day."

"Yes," agreed Cece. "I know what you mean. But you have the option of just taking off whenever you feel like it. That's fun, isn't it?"

"He should talk," said Bea. "He works hard Monday to Friday, then switches off on the weekends."

"Yes, but I'm not doing creative work like Gerry is," Cece pointed out.

But Gerry seemed to have lost interest, was fiddling with her salad.

"What is it, dear?" said Bea, leaning over and touching Gerry's hand.

Not for the first time was Gerry reminded that Bea and Cece were her parents' ages — maybe a little younger — and that she was comforted by having them to lean on. "I've been meaning to discuss this with you for some time," she began.

"Uh oh," groaned Cece. "Should I put on my lawyer hat?"

"No, no, nothing like that, though I suppose that now I have stuff, I should make a will."

"Yes, you should," he agreed.

"I'll think about it. Would you like a ramshackle old house and twenty, I mean nineteen, cats?"

They shook their heads.

Gerry sighed. "I went through all Aunt Maggie's files, papers, letters — everything."

Cece leaned forward. "Yes?"

"Everything was in order. But I found some letters pushed down, hidden. They'd not been posted, had been left at the house, I guess." She sipped her wine. "Anyway — you're the first I've told of this — they're nasty letters, full of threats and insults. How she's a stupid, selfish old woman. How nobody loves her, not even the cats. How the cats had better not wander or they'll come to a bad end. And the letters are illustrated, but so poorly. It's almost as if a kid drew them. Stick figures of cats being run over, thrown into the river in a sack. Of cats eating from dishes with skull and crossbones on them. You know, the symbol for poison? Cats with their heads cut off." She shivered. "Very nasty."

"Are they dated?" Cece queried. "Handwritten, printed?"

"Undated and typed. Except for the drawings. I'll give you them to look at, if you like. Nothing happened while Maggie was alive, did it?"

Bea spoke slowly. "Remember when we heard that the cats were sick, Cece? The winter before Maggie died."

Cece reflected. "Yeah. She said they were puking all over the place. She figured it was a bad batch of food and threw it all out. They got better."

"Oh, poor Aunt Maggie," Gerry exclaimed. "I wonder if she'd already received the letters and thought someone was trying to poison the cats."

"You should talk to Prudence," Cece advised.

Gerry shook her head. "I did and she hadn't known of the letters' existence."

"It sounds like a crank to me. I think we should have dessert and talk about Gerry's upcoming show," Bea said firmly. "Come on, drink up. I'll make coffee."

Gerry felt relieved to have shared her worries and was able to present a cheerful face to Doug next morning, despite the fact that he was there to tear apart and mend her back porch roof. "Should I stay, Doug? I trust you to do the work."

He grinned down at her where she stood under the big old apple tree. She flushed and hoped she looked cute in jean shorts, a black T and sports sandals. "No, you can go. It's a small job. I'll finish it today."

"Okay. I'll be at Cathy's if you need me." The sound of crickets followed her as she picked her way through the long grass at the side of the road. Dozens of grasshoppers zoomed out of her path, some landing briefly on her bare legs. She stifled small screams. City girl, she admonished herself.

Blue jays screeched nearby and robins hopped, pecking at all the insect life on offer. She passed Mr. Parminter's. An incurious woodpecker tapped at a tree on the lawn. She saw Graymalkin watching it from the porch. Good, good. She turned into Cathy's driveway.

As it was the weekend, she was unsurprised to see a few cars in the driveway — the B&B's paying guests — and went round the back to the kitchen door and opened it. "All right if I come in?"

Cathy, enjoying a post-breakfast coffee with Charles asleep at her feet, smiled. "Just finished feeding them. There's some apple cinnamon loaf, if you want it." She looked tired.

"I'll get it. I'll get it. Cathy, is doing the snacks for my show going to be too much?"

"When is it again?"

Gerry named the date.

"So, a little while yet, eh? What? Three weeks? I should be fine. I'm improving every day. What numbers do you expect?"

"Well, I'm inviting people all the time plus there'll be a notice in the paper so…between fifty and a hundred?"

"Oh my. If we allow at least five per person, that's two hundred and fifty to five hundred hors d'oeuvres! Oh my!" She seemed overwhelmed, then checked herself. "No, it'll be fine. Cheese straws are easy. I'll make lots of those." Gerry, who'd had them — crisp, buttery, cheddary concoctions — licked her lips. Cathy laughed. "I'll make a dozen extra for you."

"Yes, please. And those bacon-wrapped chicken livers in brandy? Are they hard?"

"No, they just have to be made on the day. So cheese straws several days ahead — a hundred of them; no, two hundred. And a hundred chicken livers. Gerry, this could get expensive."

Gerry shook her head. "I want to splash out. To thank all the people who've been helping me. You — though you'll be pooped by party time — Doug, Prudence, Cece and Bea, the Shiptons. Did I tell you I got another commission through them? Another garden. One of Mrs. Shipton's neighbours. Okay, what else?"

"We're up to three hundred. You realize if nobody comes you'll be eating this stuff for weeks?"

"Better make things I like then. What about canapés? Those are easier. Blue cheese and caramelized onions on toast squares." That burger at the Parsley had become one of Gerry's favourites.

"Yee-es. And I could prepare the toast and onions ahead of time, just run them under the broiler before serving. Better make a hundred of those. Some people don't like blue cheese."

"Fools, eh, Charles?" Gerry said to the sleeping dog. One weak thump of the tail was all he could muster.

"You'd be surprised what people don't like. I had a woman staying here turn up her nose at baked potatoes. I mean, really."

"We only need one hundred more of something."

"How about cold canapés? Chopped egg? Some with olives, some with a cherry tomato. Cheap, easy, make ahead."

"You've done it! Cost it out, pay yourself for your time and give me an estimate. If there's any left over we can serve it to the folks who come on the Saturday and Sunday after the vernissage. Which reminds me, I should go home and design the ad and buzz it over to the *Herald*." She gave Cathy a kiss. "Thank you. For doing this."

Cathy looked pleased. Charles woke up in time for a pat from Gerry.

At home, she went in the front door and to her study. As she drew the notice, she heard sounds of roofing being ripped up and thrown to the ground. She delivered the ad copy to Judith at the paper, then picked up a pizza.

"Lunch, Doug," she called as she walked back in. "Doug?" She heard a dismal gurgle from the downstairs toilet and waited anxiously till he emerged.

"Uh, it's broken, I'm afraid."

"What? Did you try plunging?"

"Mm. It's just not going down. I suspect it's to do with the weeping field. It's sodden, the tiles are broken and the water's backing up."

"And the Hudsons are busy and nobody else wants the work," Gerry responded glumly.

"They'll come eventually," Doug assured her. "They've got a development to finish and then they'll be here. Meanwhile, maybe you should make an attractive sign to put in the toilet, explaining the situation, while I get back on the roof."

"Pizza first. Then back to reality."

After lunch she made the sign, a copy of one she'd seen in the toilet of a store in town. "If it's yellow, let it mellow. If it's brown, send it down." "And pray," she added to herself. She hung it on the door of the toilet then, promising herself she was going to try and have a weekend off, or at least part of one, she retreated to the studio with Marigold and soon became engrossed in one of the family's ancient books.

Published in 1934, *Miss Buncle's Book* by D.E. Stevenson was a gentle humorous look at polite society in a small British town between the wars. Gerry fell asleep on one of the banquettes. The absence of banging hammer noise woke her.

Doug was gone. The roof was done. A few boxes of rubbish were in the driveway. He'd left a note in the kitchen. "Come for a drink at the inn if you like. Eightish." She did the cat patrol, freshened up and drove to the Parsley.

Saturday night was busier than the Friday she'd been there with Andrew had been. Nervously, she left the car in the lot, asking the boy to keep an eye on it. She went to the pub side of the building and saw Doug sitting alone.

"Well, this is nice," she said, brightly.

"I wasn't sure you'd come," he said slowly.

"I'd have called if so," she replied. "I'll have a glass of rosé, please," she told the young waitress. "All these kids who work here kind of look alike."

"That's because they're the children or other relatives of the owner — Phil Parsley."

"Any relation to Bill?"

"Brothers."

"Judy's nice."

"Yeah, great kid."

There was a pause, which Gerry broke. "Doug, you were going to tell me about your art when I rushed away to help Cathy with Prince Charles. Remember?"

He looked at her steadily. "I remember. I remember you asking about it. I don't remember whether I was going to tell you about it."

She felt taken aback and it must have shown on her face. "I'm sorry. I — "

He interrupted. "I'm just explaining how I feel. It's something addicts have to learn. Why they feel so bad they try to destroy themselves and wind up destroying everything else." She kept silent so he continued. "You ever hear that expression 'Art is sickness'?"

"No."

"Well, for some of us, who become obsessed — or maybe we become addicted to our art — art isn't a creative, regenerative act. It's destructive, frustrating." He got up and got himself another ginger ale. "I should explain.

"I was young. I was at art college. I came home one summer and there was Margaret Petherbridge. She used to be fun. We're related. Her grandmother — your grandmother — was my great-aunt. My grandmother was a Catford.

"We'd gone through school together — we're the same age — and back then there was only one class for each grade."

Gerry thought of the Toronto high school she'd attended with about ten graduating classes in her year. "Go on. There was Margaret."

"Yeah. So. We hung out at the same places — the yacht club, the golf course. Our parents knew each other. It seemed natural. And she got pregnant. I got her pregnant. With James. So we married.

"At first it was fine. I quit school, started working for her father, Geoff, at the furniture store. But I kept up my artwork on the side, or tried to. And Margaret changed, wanted her own house. Did I mention that we lived with her parents at first? Geoff's great, but her mother, Mary, what a whacko. One day, sweet as pie, the next, biting your head off. No wonder Margaret got sour. And we couldn't afford our own place. But as the other boys came along, Geoff let us have a little house he'd been renting out for profit. He let us have it for nothing.

"Well, I stuck it out for a few years, but it wasn't any good. Our marriage had been a mistake. I couldn't concentrate at work or at home. I drank too much. It got really bad for a few years. I wasn't working. I wasn't making art. Then she threw me out.

"Best thing that ever happened. I straightened out, found a room at the Parsley, got enough odd jobs to be able to give Margaret something each month and started doing art again. Want to see?"

He led her out a back door onto the sloping lawn of the inn. An intricate assemblage of metal and neon winked and shimmered, casting its reflection on the nearby lake.

"I always liked welding in high school and studied sculpture at college. One of my part-time jobs was at a neon sign factory. It all suddenly came together."

"It's gorgeous, Doug! Original, too. I've not seen anything quite like it."

They admired the piece as it glowed, various colours alternating on and off. Gerry saw his canoe pulled up on the lawn. "That's yours, isn't it, Doug?" When he nodded, she asked, "Do you ever go out in it late at night in the rain? I thought I saw someone near my house a few weeks ago."

"Wasn't me. But I may know who it was."

8

"Gerry, my dear, how are you?"

"Fine. Who is this, please?"

The voice at the other end of the line paused, its cheeriness temporarily checked. "It's your Aunt Mary," it snapped, then resumed the initial friendly tone. "I'm calling to see if you'd like to come over for a little BBQ we're having this afternoon. Just the family. For Labour Day. From two o'clock on." And before Gerry could accept or refuse, the voice said, "Bah-ee!" and hung up.

"How bizarre." Gerry hung up. "Well, I don't want to go. Do I have to go, Princess?" They were on the newly repaired back porch, Gerry reading, Marigold reclining on the floor. "It might be a distraction from the terror I'm feeling at the prospect of teaching my first art class *in three days!*" The cat started at the intensity in her voice. Gerry put the book aside.

She had five people who'd committed to the class and sent her a deposit. Her art show was three-quarters finished. She was hard at work on her next garden painting commission, and had begun discussions with a major greeting-card company to produce a line featuring *Mug the Bug*. Financially, things were improving.

But: the Hudsons still hadn't repaired the house's septic system; she still had one cat, Lightning, that was hostile; she didn't know if or when someone might begin disposing of the cats; and now she was afraid to go to a family BBQ in case she found herself outnumbered by hostile relations.

She phoned Andrew. "Are you going to your mother's this afternoon?"

"Of course. It's a tradition. Labour Day BBQ."

"Can I come with you? Maybe —" she bit off what she had been going to say, that maybe his family would back off if he stuck close to her. She compromised with, "I'm a bit nervous about being with your mother and Margaret."

He laughed. "I'll look after you."

She hoped he would. "Maybe I could pick up some wine on the way?"

"All right. See you a bit before two. I'll drive."

Gerry had a few hours to kill, so, after feeding Marigold, decided to tackle the fourth wall in the gallery. She'd been studying and researching the art at The Maples — the paintings that, presumably, her family had purchased from professional artists over the years. She went up to Aunt Maggie's office where her typewriter was and began typing up the cards she intended to mount on the wall near each piece. The little cat noiselessly followed her and sat on the desk.

A few Victorian-era landscapes or rather, seascapes, of the old country, some rather nice studies of young girls by an early twentieth-century painter, and work by local Quebec artists of the lake, the river and the house itself, seen from the water, made up the collection, or at least what she'd selected for this show. She had kept the few non-representational pieces for another time. She knew many people found abstract art off-putting.

After the typing was completed, she realized she had to decide how much she was going to charge for her *Mug the Bug* posters, the only things actually for immediate sale. And she'd need a big sign for the wall where she intended to display the portraits of Cathy's, Mr. Parminter's and the Shiptons' houses, to indicate to prospective clients that they too could possess such representations of their own buildings.

"Oops! Is that the time?" She'd heard the downstairs clock chime one. "Time to make myself beautiful." She patted Marigold and jumped into the shower.

"Will there be a lot of relatives there, Andrew?" Gerry looked at his long thin face as he concentrated on the road, and wondered again what the troubles Cathy had mentioned him having could be.

"Let's see. Margaret and the boys, of course. The Shaplands won't be there because of Doug and Margaret. And Mother offended Dad's family long ago, so no Petherbridges. Which leaves the Parsleys, and maybe Cece and Bea."

"Oh, good. If they're there, I'll have someone to talk to."

"Yes. Cece is the family lawyer, so even Mother doesn't cross him. And the Parsleys are so prominent, she likes to keep on their good sides."

He sounded so matter-of-fact describing his mother's self-serving behaviour that Gerry decided commiseration would be rude and just changed the subject. "I'm looking forward to seeing their lovely home again. It's been years since I was there." She stopped, remembering how Aunt Mary hadn't liked Gerry's mother, and wondered if the woman had any friends.

"It's Mother's pride and joy. Dad would have been happy to stay in his family home where we all grew up, but Mother wanted something bigger, showier, so they built this one near the golf club." As he spoke, they pulled into the long circular drive.

The house was white stucco with dark brown, mock-Tudor beams stuck on the outside walls, and a matching Tudor-style roof. Broad steps led up to the front door, which was double-wide and studded with bolts holding large flat hasps. The front garden was formal. Pairs of shrubs accentuated a pathway that led to a large fountain in the centre of the lawn.

They walked around the side of the house through a trellised gate where late roses and clematis twined up and over. A vast expanse of lawn was broken up by a huge pool, where Margaret's two oldest boys were swimming, with a lot of decking across the back of the house.

"Andrew!" cried Mary enthusiastically from her spot on a canvas-roofed swing chair. Margaret was seated next to her, and across from them, to Gerry's relief, were Cece and Bea.

Andrew kissed his mother and his sister and greeted the Muxworthys.

"And Gerry," added Mary with somewhat less enthusiasm. Gerry gave everyone a kiss. Cece climbed out of the chair to give Gerry his spot.

"Shall I take drink orders, ladies?" he asked.

"I'll help you," said Andrew. "Dad in the house?"

"Watching his golf," said Mary. Both men disappeared into the back of the house, only Cece reappearing with their drinks before rejoining the rest of the men inside.

"We won't see them for a while," snorted Mary. "Cheers." She set the swing in motion.

Gerry sipped her wine. "You have a lovely home, Aunt Mary."

"It's not bad," Mary admitted in a bored voice. "Not bad. The best Geoff could do, I suppose."

Margaret looked a bit embarrassed and Gerry almost felt sorry for her. As the swing went faster, she gamely carried on, finding it difficult to drink her wine without banging her teeth against the glass. "Do you garden yourself or have help?"

"Oh, help, you know. But just because I have a gardener doesn't mean I don't know about plants." She spoke tartly, then tried to recover her poise. "For example, those are foxgloves, and Shasta daisies, that's datura, and next to the aconite are hollyhocks."

"I've seen all of those in Aunt Maggie's garden," Gerry replied politely. Plants were safe. They could talk about plants.

"Well, sisters, you know. We'd share plants. A cutting of this, some seedlings." She put out a foot and a hand and the swing braked sharply. They all protected their drinks. "Margaret, get us some snacks, there's a love."

Margaret rose to do her mother's bidding. "And while you're in there, you might like to make a salad or something, to go with the meat."

Margaret, with a face that threatened an angry remark, silently went away. "I'm useless in the kitchen," Mary tinkled. "Absolutely useless. Bea, how are you? How's the condition?" Mary had switched to tones of empathy so false-sounding Gerry caught her breath.

Bea replied mildly. "Some days are good. This is one of them. I'm happy to be here." And saluted her hostess with her drink.

But Mary wouldn't leave it alone. "Such a serious condition, potentially, I mean. I mean, you've a long way to go." She switched her gaze to Gerry. "And Cece is so good to her. We all marvel. Was a time we thought he might be interested in Margaret, but then she met Doug and he met Bea."

She's got no filters at all, thought a scandalized Gerry. Margaret picked that moment to rejoin them with a bowl of chips and some dip. "Thank you, honey. You're so good to me." Mary rewarded her daughter with a bright smile. "Bring Mum a fresh drink, darling."

And so it went. No Parsleys ever showed, and Gerry could only admire their decision.

Uncle Geoff finally appeared and grilled some chicken, some meat. "No shrimp?" Mary commented as her husband brought her a plate. The boys jumped out of the pool and the rest of the men came outside. Gerry was glad to see David, took him aside for a moment.

"How are you?" He mumbled something. "Your dad told me you like to canoe on the river when you're sleeping over at his place." She said nothing about the scare she'd received when he'd taken his midnight tour past her house. "You know, you can canoe over to see Bob anytime," she began to say, but remembering her skinny-dipping, amended that statement. "Actually, I might be working, so better phone first, but most days I'm there and Bob's always there. Are you going back to school this week?"

He nodded and at this point his brothers called him away. They'd only briefly addressed her all afternoon and she imagined there was pressure on them and him to maintain Margaret and Mary's coolness.

With relief, she turned to Andrew, who was balancing a plate piled with steak, corn on the cob and potato salad. "Is that for me?" she teased.

"Why? Do you want it?"

"No, I'm kidding. I want chicken, I think. Hey, do you call leaving me with Margaret and your mother looking after me?"

"You had Bea there and I think you're tougher than you look."

"You're right. I am. But I still want to eat my dinner with you, so guard this chair. I'll be back." As she was serving herself from the buffet set up on the deck, she overheard Margaret finishing a thought.

"...probably wrote them herself so she can get rid of the animals in the future." Gerry turned and stared at her cousin hard. Margaret, who'd been talking with her mother, turned a bright crimson and ducked into the kitchen. Gerry followed. Mary laughed and turned away to talk to somebody else.

"Margaret, were you speaking about me just now? About some letters, about Aunt Maggie's cats?"

"No," Margaret said stubbornly.

"Because, if you were, I'd be very interested to know how you know about them."

Margaret was silent, opened the fridge as if looking for something. Gerry gave up and went back to eat with Andrew. Her cheeks felt hot and she had tears in her eyes but Andrew appeared not to notice. "Good?" he asked, pointing his knife at her plate.

"What? Oh, yeah. Delicious."

After everyone had eaten, the event just kind of petered out. Andrew drove her home, they quietly said good night, and a shattered Gerry thankfully let herself into her home, fed her cats and crawled into bed early with a book and a cup of tea.

9

Monday morning, it was as if the cats knew Gerry was exhausted. They let her sleep in an extra half hour before Bob began kneading her leg with his sharp little pins and Marigold became restless.

Gerry opened her eyes and stared at the ceiling. Could yesterday really have happened? Was there a rumour that she, Gerry, had fabricated the poison pen letters as a way of preparing for the sudden demise of the cats? And, if so, had her cousin Margaret started the rumour?

She stroked Marigold with one hand and played with Bob with the other. "What happened here, guys, to create so much bad feeling? Even now Aunt Maggie is dead."

The cats stretched and Bob ran to the door. "I know, I know. Tummies first," said Gerry, dragging herself down to her chores.

Though it was Labour Day, Prudence was coming, as they wanted to do some baking for the art class on Wednesday. Correction: Gerry had assumed Prudence would do any necessary baking, while Prudence had indicated it was a fine opportunity for Gerry to learn how to bake herself. Gerry fed the cats and had just tidied up when Prudence arrived, lugging two bags of baking supplies. "Cookies and squares," she announced. "Easy to make and they'll keep in tins."

Gerry ate her toast as she watched Prudence lay out her purchases. "All the wet ingredients in one bowl. All the dry in another. Whisk."

"Why couldn't I serve store-bought cookies again?" a disgruntled Gerry asked.

"Cuts into the profits, number one. Number two — you have the pride of the Coneybears to maintain."

Gerry whisked the wet ingredients, then paused. "Oh. I should have whisked the dry first."

"Just wash the whisk and dry it well."

"Prudence, speaking of the pride of the Coneybears, I haven't had a chance to look at the family genealogy again. Where do you fit in? Aren't you part Coneybear?"

"No, I'm mostly Catford and Parsley, as far as I know. My mother, Constance Parsley, married Edward Catford, who was your grandmother Ellie Catford Coneybear's brother."

"That's right. I'd forgotten Gramma Ellie was your aunt. So you and Aunt Maggie are, were, cousins. Which makes you my... second cousin?"

Prudence smiled. "Something like that. Are you ready to mix the dry into the wet?"

Gerry was excited. "Ready? Ready? Yes, I'm ready!" She dumped the dry mixture into the wet and began whisking. Flour spurted everywhere. Patiently, Prudence removed the whisk, replacing it with a wooden spoon.

"Here, my dear, this will work much better."

Gerry beat the mixture until it was nice and smooth and fluffy. "What are we making, by the way?"

"Chocolate chip cookies," said Prudence, dumping in a whole bag of semi-sweet chocolate chips. "Recipe's on the bag. Easy, ain't it?"

When cookies were cooling on racks, and a pan of blondies ("A kind of butterscotch brownie.") was tantalizing with its warm smell, Gerry vented about Mary's BBQ. "It was horrible, Prudence. I never want to see those two women again."

They each took a cookie and a cup of tea and went to sit on the back porch.

"See them only a few times a year, I guess. When you absolutely can't avoid it."

"You mean like Christmas and other holidays?"

"Exactly."

"Well, all I can say is, don't be surprised if you hear I have the twenty-four-hour flu this Christmas — whoa, Marigold! What are you doing?"

The cat had pushed Prudence's teacup over, so the tea sloshed into the saucer and onto the table. Gerry ran to the kitchen for some paper towels and a wet rag. When she returned, Prudence was examining what remained of her tea. She had a strange look on her face. "Gerry, look!"

Gerry peered into the cup. "A wasp! It's still struggling. That wouldn't have been very nice to drink. How did that get into there?"

Prudence seemed distracted as she opened the screen door and threw the wasp into the garden. It sat on the flagstone path, presumably dripping tea and catching its breath. Prudence seemed distracted. "Oh, there must be a hole in the screen somewhere. The wasps go a bit mental at summer's end. But — "

"What?"

"Shush. I'm thinking." She looked at Marigold, still on the table, now grooming a paw. "She did this once before, Gerry. The awful morning I found your aunt."

"She tipped over a teacup?"

Prudence nodded. "I already had a bad feeling when I arrived. The garbage hadn't been put at the curb. I did that, then went in the house. I called for your aunt. She usually had the coffee on by the time I arrived and sometimes had already fed the cats. I went through into the dining room. The cats were all sitting very quietly on their chairs. That's when I knew something was wrong.

"I ran up the stairs, calling, but there was no reply. Bob ran away. He'd been at the door of Maggie's room. I went inside and... there she was. The four usual cats were still at the foot of the bed.

Marigold was lying curled in the curve of Maggie's belly, but when I started shouting and shaking Maggie, Marigold jumped to the night table, looked me in the face, put out a paw, and knocked over the teacup.

"I must confess, I shouted at Marigold. 'Stupid cat! What did you do that for?' And I took a swipe at her. Then I ran downstairs and called Andrew and he called the police. They all arrived — the firefighters, and the emergency workers. But she'd been dead for hours. It was obvious."

"Let me make you another cup of tea," Gerry gently suggested.

"Later. I've never told anyone this before, except Mother, of course, and Mrs. Smith. An ambulance came and took Maggie away, and I was so shocked I just did what I always do. I fed the cats, cleaned out the cat boxes. And then I went upstairs and changed the sheets. I wiped up the spilt tea, but before I washed the teacup, I happened to notice what was left of the tea. It was a pale greenish yellow. And Gerry — " she turned her face to look urgently in Gerry's eyes — "she hadn't put any milk in it."

"So?"

"So she always took milk and sometimes sugar. I looked in the fridge and there was milk there."

"What about herbal tea? Some people don't add anything to them."

"She hated herbal teas, only drank black tea, well-brewed."

"And you didn't tell anyone?"

"I was in shock, I guess, at the time. And the cause of death was said to be heart failure. She was cremated and buried and by then it was too late to accuse someone…"

"Someone of poisoning her. You think Marigold tipped over the teacup to show you there was something dangerous inside. Like the wasp."

Marigold had finished grooming, delicately picked her way between the sodden paper towels and cups over to Gerry, hopped down off the table into her lap, kneaded a bit, curled and closed her eyes. Both women stared at her, their mouths open.

"Tell no one about this," cautioned Prudence. "They'll think I'm senile and you're a crazy cat lady."

Gerry nodded, her brain fizzing with possibilities. The kitchen timer buzzed and they both jumped before Prudence went to check the blondies. Gerry sat and finished her tea, gazing blankly at nothing. Somewhere, a wasp buzzed.

Gerry added a little black to the white pigment and played with it until she got the desired grey. Once again, she was working at the puzzle of how to paint white. The flower, a perfect example of *Datura suaveolens*, or Angel's Trumpet, rested in a vase on a small table in the bamboo room. She wanted the demarcation between the gold bamboo of the wall below and the pale green painted wall above to be exactly two-thirds of the way up the finished composition.

She was absorbed in her task. The house was silent. A little blue now, she thought, and reached for the tube, when — beep, beep, beep, beep — there was the sound of wood cracking, a shouted "Stop!" She heard men's voices murmuring and an idling motor.

"What the — ?" She put down the paint and peered out the front window, but the ivy got in the way. All she could see was part of a large yellow object. "Oh, my God, there's been an accident!" She rushed out the front door of the house.

Her white wooden fence was gone, under the backhoe, which partially blocked the road. Two giant men, one middle-aged, one young, stood looking at her sheepishly. A pickup truck was parked on the shoulder across the road, further impeding traffic. Cars inched through the narrow gap along the centre line, their drivers glaring.

"Hoo-boy," she said. "Hudsons, I presume?"

They nodded. The younger one mounted the backhoe and began to reverse while his elder halted traffic. Gerry couldn't bear to watch. She hoped they had insurance, because they owed her a fence. Grimly, she went inside.

She spent the day counting cats. She blocked the cat flap, trying to keep them inside. Lightning, the mostly black calico with the blaze running down her savage-looking nose, was particularly incensed. Suspecting a trap, she put her ears back and hissed at Gerry and the other cats alike. Finally, Gerry chased her with a broom into the little kitchen and stood looking down at the demented creature. "Right!" she bellowed. "I've had enough of you. We're going to sort this out right now, or by God, I'm going to throw you under the backhoe!"

Appalled at herself, Gerry stopped yelling and dropped the broom. The backhoe sounded as if it was next going to come through a wall of the house. Gerry crouched and took a good look at the beast, backed into a corner. "So, you're a calico like the Princess out there, which means you probably need to be Top Cat, but she's already it, so you're frustrated. I can understand that. What did Aunt Maggie see when she looked at you?"

Gerry looked into the cat's eyes and penetrated past the anger, the wildness, to a sad and lonely place. "Oh, kitten, I'm sorry. Here, have some of Marigold's chicken." She put a bit on a plate and pushed it toward the cat. It ate, growling the whole time, and she got a good look at its tail.

There wasn't much more than a flap of fur covering deep scars that ran down from the base of her spine to her back feet. The scars were white and the fur hadn't grown back. "Oh, sweetie, I'm so sorry for you. You had a bad injury once, I see that. I promise I'll be more patient." Gerry opened the kitchen door and the cat scooted back into the living room.

"Wow! I'm glad nobody witnessed that. I almost killed one of the cats, fulfilling part of Margaret's rumour." She made herself lunch and automatically went to the back porch to eat it.

The work of ripping up a quarter of her lawn had ceased, and the Hudsons were peering into the hole. What now? Gerry thought, and walked around to where they were looking. The older Hudson croaked, "A tiny hand," and Gerry felt her heart jolt. Had they found a dead baby buried in her garden? She looked fearfully down in the hole.

"Where?" she said tremulously. Hudson Sr. pointed and she followed the direction. There, as if waving from an earthen grave, was a ceramic hand, about a half inch long. "Oh, for heaven's sake!" said Gerry, "Just dig it out. It broke and someone threw it away."

Hudson Jr. jumped into the hole and stuck one enormous hand into the muck under the ceramic. He lifted, and through the ooze they could see the lady was intact. They hosed her off and then, and only then, Gerry picked her up. It was Royal Doulton — a Highland lassie in a cream dress, with a green tartan plaid flung over one shoulder. "Well, I'll be," said Gerry.

The men got back to work while Gerry walked slowly back to her uneaten lunch, turning the figurine over and over. It didn't make sense. Why would someone bury a perfectly good object?

Back in her studio, she put the lady on the mantel and tried to concentrate on her painting. She was already thinking ahead to a spring show when she'd have more work for sale. Flower portraits were one of the things she thought might sell. People might like them for their bedrooms, even a bathroom. Which reminded her.

Outside again, she waved at Hudson Sr. and he came over. "When will you be finished?"

"What?" He cupped his ear.

"Finished. When?" she shouted.

"Oh. Drop the tank tomorrow, cover it up. Three, four o'clock tomorrow?"

Gerry smiled at him through gritted teeth. "Thank you." Of course. The backhoe would be grinding tomorrow afternoon all during her first art class.

She went inside and removed a blondie from a tin. Damn, these were good!

The gods of the arts must have taken pity on her because she woke at seven the next morning to the beep, beep, beep, beep of something large being backed onto her property. She leaned out of her bedroom's front window. A big flatbed holding a weird giant container was jackknifed, as its driver attempted his manoeuvre. The Hudsons were directing him, while traffic was stopped both ways.

Gerry quickly withdrew her head. "Nothing to do with me," she said to the cats. "Let them get on with it." She'd finished the cat chores when Prudence arrived.

"Good thing I walk, otherwise I'd be waiting down by the church hall, traffic's so backed up!" She got the vacuum cleaner from the cupboard under the servants' stairs and set to.

Gerry took her coffee into her studio and did a final tidy, all the while assessing the noise level happening a few feet beyond the room's wall, mostly men shouting and the hum of the flatbed's motor. Caught between that and the vacuum cleaner's drone, and unable to go outside, the cats were jumpy. "One more day, guys, I promise, then things should be back to normal."

She decided to offer her students several objects to sketch. She hoped Marigold would honour the class with her presence but that was out of her control. She arranged the Royal Doulton lady, the vase of datura, a pile of old books, and a pair of candlesticks on the room's mantel, and placed six chairs in a semi-circle facing that. She, too, would sketch, rising from time to time to observe and comment.

The sound of the vacuum cleaner had stopped and she heard — nothing but the birds and insects outside her window. She went for a cautious look.

The Hudsons' early start had paid off. The tank was in, the soil had been backfilled around it, and they were gone. Prudence joined her and they ruefully looked at the ruined half of the yard. What was left of the fence was stacked in one corner. Part of the perennial garden was gone and the ground, though flattish, was uneven, sandy in some spots, packed clay in others. "The cats are going to track all that into the house," Prudence observed grimly.

"Keep them in for the rest of today. After the class is over, it doesn't matter. Meanwhile, I'm going to call Doug. I've got to get this fixed up quick."

"Meanwhile," said Prudence, "you have one hour to eat and change and then you're teaching. I'll call Doug. We need topsoil and turf and a new fence. Right?"

"Right," said Gerry, and dashed away, pausing only to flush the downstairs toilet and yell "Yay!" before rushing upstairs to shower. She grabbed a sandwich and was sweeping construction mud and gravel off the front driveway when the first student arrived. "Hellooo," she said graciously and showed them where to park.

Judy Parsley she knew, of course, but the others were strangers. Christine Carder, a tall old lady with a stiff neck and white hair beautifully piled on her head, introduced herself as having known Aunt Maggie quite well and wasn't it a shame she'd died so young. Fifty-five is maybe still middle age, thought Gerry, but it's certainly not young!

The next two arrived together, a pair of late middle-aged ladies with nicely dyed hairdos and immaculate makeup. Gerry vaguely recognized them from around the village. They were friends: Doris Pirrie and Gladys Knill.

She was just shepherding them in the front door when a smart car drove up and out jumped a short thin man, balding, with glasses. "Sorry, sorry. Almost late. Ben Lymbery. Ben Lymbery. Ben Lymbery." He repeated his name to each person with whom he shook hands, and when he got to Gerry the second time, she called a halt.

"If you'd like to go through, we're just to the right."

There were "oos" and "ahs" of pleasure and admiration as they filed into the majestic, dark entranceway and then the cool, bright studio and took their seats. Gerry stood in front of the fireplace. "I'm Gerry Coneybear and I'm really happy to welcome you to your first art lesson — with me, that is. I know Judy has taken art before. Anyone else?" The ladies shook their heads. "Mr. Lymbery?"

"I took an evening class at the junior college a few years back but didn't enjoy the night driving."

Gerry paused, waiting to hear if he had anything further to say that was pertinent to art. He didn't. "Well," she continued brightly, "no night driving here. Everyone got their sketch pads and pencils?" They held them up. "Perfect." She stepped to one side, revealing the massed objects behind her. "Let's begin."

An hour and a half later there was a gentle tap at the door. Gerry clapped her hands. "If you would like some refreshments for, say, fifteen minutes, please follow me." They moved back into the foyer, past the downstairs bathroom and through the screen door onto the porch. More gasps of pleasure ensued when they saw the back garden, the lake, the far shore. "At a future lesson, I'd like us to sit on the lawn and sketch this view," she said, quickly taking two blondies and a cup of tea.

"How marvellous," said Christine, "that you're continuing the tradition of Coneybears at The Maples."

"Oh, there's no shortage of Coneybears," mumbled Gerry, her mouth full of blondie.

"But living here, keeping such a big old house going — it's a great undertaking." Christine looked worried.

"I understand that, Christine, and I'll do my best." Christine seemed satisfied and took a cookie.

"Did you bake these?" asked Doris. "They're really good."

Gerry nodded. Ben piped up, "A woman of many talents." Gerry smiled graciously. It was really going very well.

At the end of the class, she knew what she had. Judy and Christine had some innate talent; the other three would have to be coaxed along. They seemed happy enough and it was a triumphant Gerry who helped Prudence feed the cats at the end of the day. "You were right about the baking, Prudence. They loved it. What shall we make next week?"

Prudence smiled. "Cake."

PART 3

HORTICULTURE

First Cat woke slowly, hearing a familiar voice. She uncurled from her position next to the young woman's chest and stretched. She looked past a sleeping Second Cat to the bedroom doorway. The other woman, the first woman, stood there smiling and beckoning.

First Cat jumped off the bed and followed her downstairs and through the dining room. A few of the sleeping cats stirred, the fur rising on their backs, but when they saw who it was, they relaxed.

The cat pushed through the cat flap and into the garden as the woman melted through the wall. A heavy dew was on the lawn and the woman laughed silently to see the little cat lift and shake each wet paw fastidiously.

They walked up and down the various paths through the perennial garden. The woman paused to inspect where fresh sod had been laid over the broken ground. A sprinkler flicked water, keeping the grass alive.

She seemed perplexed by the slight reconfiguration of the perennial beds and paused, searching. First Cat sat on a flagstone near the sundial and watched.

The woman made her decision, stood, or floated rather, by one particular plant, one of the ones First Cat had sniffed at earlier that summer. The woman pointed and made first digging, then pulling motions with her hands.

First Cat began to dig around the plant. It was tall with violet-blue flowers that looked as misty and insubstantial as the woman.

Her illness made her weak and she had to stop and rest several times, though the woman urged her on.

Finally, she felt the roots give, and the plant slowly toppled over.

The woman seemed satisfied, made stroking motions with her hands, her mouth smiling and appearing to say the cat's name. The little cat arched her thin back, hoping to feel the familiar caress, but the woman walked away down the lawn, drifted above the rocky shore and onto the water, where she became just another ripple on the surface of the lake.

The cat, covered in mud, sat by the plant and howled.

10

Somehow Doug had wangled a load of topsoil to be delivered the day after the art class, and he and Gerry had spent the afternoon spreading it as evenly as possible while Bob, the boys, and assorted cats zoomed in and out of the mess, stimulated by the sudden change in the topography. The more cautious cats sniffed around the edges of the work area. The day after that the sod arrived, and they'd worked hard again unrolling it and pushing one strip tight up against the other. Gerry, who saw money evaporating before her eyes, begged Doug to tell her how to repair the part of the garden that was wrecked, and he explained about lifting perennials, splitting the roots and shifting the plants around.

"See, all these day lilies, all these purple cone flowers — big plants — can be divided into four or five new plants. The phlox too. It's not difficult, just hard work."

"I'll do it this weekend," sighed Gerry, enjoying an iced tea while sitting sprawled on the lawn. Her clothes and rubber boots too filthy to allow her in the house, she'd left drinks and snacks on the kitchen porch.

"Just remember to water the hole before you plant, and then water the plants every day for about a week. The days are cooler now, so they should be fine."

"Okay. Thank goodness the art show is still two weeks off. Maybe the landscape will be relatively restored by then. I was meaning to ask you, would you like to exhibit a piece of your art outside? I think it would be neat to look out the windows at night and see neon on the lawn."

Doug frowned. "I have some small pieces ready, prototypes, but nothing large."

"We could put them on pedestals, say, the sundial, or on rocks by the water's edge."

"I'll think about it, and thank you for asking. I'd better get going."

"Thanks for all your help. I hope this is the end of my string of house disasters."

He laughed. "Old house, new house. There's always something. Bye, Gerry." He got into his canoe and paddled away.

She rose and surveyed all their hard work. She'd enjoyed it, mostly, but especially enjoyed the thought of the hot bath that was to be her reward. She shed most of her clothes outside the backyard screened porch and padded in bare feet, shirt and underpants into the house and upstairs. As she soaked, her mind returned to thinking about the teacups Marigold had knocked over. It was like pressing on a sore tooth with her tongue; whenever she wasn't distracted, she found her thoughts going there.

Marigold was not a whimsical cat. If it had been Bob tipping teacups, Gerry would have put it down to his sense of humour and switched to using only mugs.

But Marigold was a serious cat, undistracted by catnip mice, crumpled aluminum foil balls, or even the moths and crickets that the other cats batted at or chased. If she tipped two teacups, she had a reason, possibly two reasons.

Both times, she had been trying to show Prudence something. And Prudence had noticed, but it had only had real meaning after Marigold tipped the second cup.

Both women had agreed that it might mean there was something wrong with Maggie's last cup of tea. But what?

Gerry sighed. They didn't have enough information and really no idea as to what to do next. They'd agreed to wait and think, but not to forget.

She spent Saturday in gardening clothes, thinking about colours as she shifted the yellows, purples, creams and whites around. It was soothing, creative and unbelievably time-consuming, as well as tiring, but she finished late afternoon, and called Cathy to see if there was room for one more at her dinner table.

Cathy sounded harassed. "I'm sorry, Gerry. I'm doing a candlelight supper for two, for a couple who are staying here, and my cheese and spinach soufflé just collapsed."

"Oh, I understand, Cathy. Sorry to bother you." Gerry stood with the phone in her hand, looking across the road. Andrew's car was parked there, so he was probably at home. She hesitated.

She hadn't felt good about Andrew since the horrible BBQ. He'd left her alone with his female relations, despite her expressing doubts about them. He must really loathe his mother; though, judging by the fact that he'd invited Margaret out to eat, he must still be trying with her. Who was she to judge? She had no siblings. She rehung the phone on its receiver and rooted in the fridge. A sandwich, a few cookies. And there was always the pile of papers waiting upstairs in the office.

"No," she said aloud. "It's Saturday night. I am not doing the accounting. I am going to eat and read in bed and then enjoy an early night." The phone rang. It was Andrew.

"I've got a rotisserie chicken with fries, Gerry, and I remember you like chicken. Would you share it with me?"

"I'll be right there." Huh, she thought as she washed and dressed. That was an about-face I just made there. Living out here in the country must make people desperate for company. She was changed and across the road in ten minutes.

Andrew had on jeans and loafers, an open-necked, long-sleeved plaid shirt, and — a frilly pink apron. Nothing to me what he wears, thought Gerry. "Smells good in here."

"I popped it in the oven to reheat for a moment. Would you like some wine?" He led the way through the living room with its rows of Aunt Maggie's figurines all shiny in their glass cases. Mentally, Gerry shrugged. If it makes him happy.

But she liked his kitchen: white cabinets with old-fashioned details and antique hardware; the table a chunky round one on a central pedestal; the matching captain's chairs cheerful with Mediterranean blue cushions. The floor was terracotta tiles and the walls Tuscan yellow. Many plants clustered by the bow window near the table. She exclaimed, "Oh, Andrew, what a lovely kitchen! Did you design it?"

He blushed with pleasure. "I did. Do you like the colours? I read a lot of these." He gestured towards a stack of design magazines in a neat pile on one chair.

She suddenly felt sorry for him, sitting eating his dinner alone, thumbing through décor mags. But then remembered, he's in the furniture business, so maybe it's not just his occupation but his passion. After all, I live alone, her inner voice murmured. But I'm not almost forty, the same voice replied. "How old are you, Andrew?"

"I'll be thirty-eight in November."

"I'll be twenty-six in February," Gerry confided. "Twenty-five is such a nice round number. I'll be sorry to leave it. I don't know why I think that." You're babbling, she cautioned herself. He handed her a glass of white wine, then bent his tall frame in front of the oven.

"You should get one of those built-in-the-wall models, Andrew, so you don't have to bend so far."

"This oven came with the house. Maybe when it needs replacing." He served them their supper, removing the apron with a muttered, "One of Mother's."

"Andrew, what do you know about a Royal Doulton figure, one of the ladies, a Scottish lassie in cream and green?"

"Flower of Scotland. HN 4240. Isn't it a blue and white dress? The plaid is green."

"Uh, yeah, I guess so. The bodice is blue with white flowers, but the sleeves and skirt are white."

"Designed by Nada Pedley. Only been issued in the last few years."

Gerry was disappointed. "Oh, so it's not old?"

Andrew laughed. "They don't have to be old to be valuable."

"What's it worth?"

"A hundred. Hundred and fifty. Why? Did you find it?"

"Why do you ask?" Gerry said slowly, feeling the food go dry in her mouth.

"Because I gave it to Aunt Maggie for Christmas last year and I noticed it was missing from her collection when we moved it."

"Oh, you noticed that, did you?"

"Yes. Why? Is something wrong?"

"The Hudsons found it buried in the side lawn when they dug out the septic."

Andrew busied himself with his meal. "Well, I wonder how it got there?"

"I don't know. It's bizarre. I thought, if it was old, maybe it had been there a long time. May I have some more wine, please?"

He poured. "What does Prudence say?"

"I haven't asked her yet. I've been trying to put my side yard back in order."

"Is it all right — the figurine? Not chipped or scratched?"

"No, no. It's fine. I suppose it's yours."

"You can keep it, if you like it."

"I do rather like it. It's more casual than some of the other ones in their big dresses and hats. Thank you, Andrew. I will keep it."

Then he spoiled his generous offer somewhat by adding, "I can always get another one."

She didn't stay much longer. After he showed her the collections in the living room, there didn't seem much to say.

Sunday, while she was feeding the cats, she heard the bells of St. Anne's bidding the faithful to worship, and, on a whim, made herself presentable in a skirt and summer sweater and walked quickly to the church.

She was in time to join in on the last verse of the first hymn ("Holy, Holy, Holy") and settled down to listen with half of her attention, while with the other half she gazed around the church.

Yellowish walls and thick dark brown beams reminded her of Mary and Geoff Petherbridge's house, but only fleetingly. She looked at the amazing ancient stained-glass windows, huge ones at either end of the church, as well as the smaller ones set regularly in the side walls. The morning light shining through all that coloured glass bathed the congregation in an amber glow. The responses were quite relaxing to participate in, made her feel nostalgic for a time when she was young, and her parents and Aunt Maggie were alive.

Another hymn. "All Things Bright and Beautiful." Gerry looked around. There were a few children attending. Perhaps the cheerful hymn selection was for their benefit. The minister mounted the tiny pulpit for the sermon and Gerry read the brass plaques on the wall next to her head. One for the village men killed in the First World War. Alfred Coneybear 1899–1915. Poor fellow. Only sixteen. Younger than David. Another plaque for the Second World War. Andrew Catford 1921–1941. Her father's uncle. Well, at least he made it out of his teens. Barely.

There was the plaque enumerating the ancient dead of the Parsleys. The Parsleys had been the first to arrive from Devon. Then another plaque that listed the families who donated money, land or materials to build St. Anne's. Coneybears, Muxworthys, Parsleys, Catfords, Petherbridges. All the old families.

She looked around, spotted a woman seated with some of the kids who worked at the inn. Parsleys?

Another hymn, this one for the collection plate's going around. Gerry fumbled in her purse. Thank goodness. She placed the five-dollar bill on top of a pile of small white envelopes. Oh, yes. That's what regulars did, she remembered, for tax purposes.

A few more prayers. The final hymn. Then the minister processed out, ready to greet her congregation. She held Gerry's hand as she extracted her name and said how welcome she was. Gerry, embarrassed, knowing full well she'd not be making a regular appearance, muttered something about visiting her loved ones, and escaped into the cemetery.

She walked to the back, touched the three plaques as she always did, then edged around the little group milling outside the front door and walked home.

She spent the rest of the day peacefully finishing her painting of the datura bloom and beginning the portrait of Mitzi. She was enjoying a rare, for her, gin and tonic on the porch with Marigold, reading her book, looking up from time to time to take in the view, when a thought occurred.

Taking one of her largest sketchpads, she went out to the garage and placed a stool in front of the family tree. "Why am I always having to run out here to check something about the people Aunt Maggie painted?" she asked Mother, who with Ronald and the honour guard had followed her there.

She quickly copied the genealogy onto two adjacent pages, then returned to the porch. "You didn't follow me, sweetheart?" Marigold lifted a shrunken head and gazed dully at Gerry. "You're not feeling well, are you?" She gently stroked the fur between her ears until Marigold went back to sleep. Gerry studied her family tree.

It was easiest to begin with the latest generation and work backward through people she'd known, then people she'd heard about, to the fourth and fifth generations before her, who nobody living remembered. It was a sobering thought, that one day she and all the people she knew would be names on a piece of paper, on a cemetery wall.

She turned her attention to the tree, counted all the Parsleys. The name Mary reappeared frequently. There was Prudence, born in 1948, only child of Constance Parsley and Edward Catford. Alexander Crick was her husband's name. There was no death date for him. Could he still be alive? Or no, she remembered, the tree wasn't up to date. Two sad words appeared under his and Prudence's names: no issue.

There was Andrew. He'd probably been named for the uncle who'd died in the Second World War, his grandmother's brother. Had Aunt Mary been trying to curry favour with her own mother? Had she named Margaret for the same reason — to ingratiate the child with Mary's sister Margaret? Or was Gerry just being overly cynical?

She was interested to see, among the Victorian ancestors, how often a man was ten or twenty years older than his wife. Less frequently, a wife would be a few years older than her husband, usually when she married in her thirties, an old maid getting a last chance.

For example, the first Coneybear, John, born in Devon in the early 1800s, was twenty-seven years older than his wife, Sybil Muxworthy. Twenty-seven years! Even Cece Muxworthy (who Gerry didn't believe had ever given her cousin a second thought) was only about fifteen years older than Margaret. Twenty-seven years was almost two generations apart, if you considered most women were married and mothers in their late teens.

Sybil had had a daughter, Margaret, and a son, Albert, ten years apart, and in between a sad list of children who'd died in infancy. And she herself had died at twenty-eight, on or after the birth of her son, who'd be Gerry's great-grandfather.

At the other end of the longevity spectrum, Gerry noted her two great-aunts, both of whom she remembered: Sylvia and Mary, her Gramma Ellie's sisters. They'd each had half a dozen children or so and lived to be eighty-one and eighty-nine.

What a difference a hundred years made, Gerry mused, in the health of women and children. Gramma Ellie had died at fifty-six, her son Gerald (Gerry's dad) at sixty-two, and her daughter, Aunt Maggie, at fifty-five. Heart, lungs, heart. It seemed Ellie had passed down a congenital heart disease to Maggie, according to the murmurs she'd heard at the funeral. Someone had talked to her doctor, they said, who'd confirmed this.

Looking at the tree made her a bit sad. She filled in the missing death dates where she knew them, hesitating over Alexander Crick's name. Prudence must surely know. Somehow, she didn't like to ask.

Gerry woke with a start. Something was missing. She felt the lump that was Bob between her feet but the other lump, the one that seemed to creep to her for warmth, was gone.

She prowled the house, gently calling, "Marigold. Princess. Where are you?" Oh, God, she thought, remembering Prudence's remark, I really am turning into a crazy cat lady.

She padded into the kitchen. No. She backtracked and investigated the cat boxes. Somebody was scratching in one of them but it was a white somebody. It jumped out of the box and skittered past Gerry. "Back to Mother, Ronald." That left outside.

It was a dark night, so Gerry went back to the kitchen to get a flashlight. She'd just located one and was slipping on her rubber boots when she heard a howl that stopped her cold. "She's dying, or being eaten by something!" She grabbed the broom, flicked on the light and went out.

She shone the light around the parking pad, looking for a raccoon or fox, then turned and shone it the other way, on the stone path along the back of the house. There was another "Yeow!" and this time she realized it was a cat, not a wild animal.

Lightning sprang out in front of her feet, giving her a fright, then dashed across the lawn, away from the garden.

Gerry went down the stone steps and onto the lawn. She turned, searching with the light in all directions, waited to hear another cry. It came. This way.

She moved cautiously to the right, looked up at the screened back porch. Instead of her sunny refuge for morning coffee, afternoon tea or pre-dinner drink, it looked cold and damp, presented a blank face to the lake. She shivered, and pointed her light at the perennial garden.

Something moved and Gerry almost dropped the light, but it was a cat-sized something so she moved closer, praying, not a skunk, please, not a skunk.

She reached the animal and it gave a tired mew. "Oh, Princess, I found you." The little cat crouched next to an uprooted plant, and when Gerry picked her up she pressed close, hooking her claws into the shoulder of Gerry's robe. "There, there. I've got you."

Is she becoming senile? thought Gerry. Did she forget where the cat boxes are and wander outside? It was only when she got the cat inside and turned on a light that she saw how filthy she was. Wetting a dishrag, she sponged her off, then wrapped her in a towel, brought her back to bed.

Bob stretched, showing the inside of his pink mouth as they settled back down. "What good are you, Bob?" Gerry teased. "We could be in the river and you'd snore on." He blinked at her placidly and groomed his shoulder. Marigold was already asleep.

11

Gerry didn't get much artwork done that week, found herself working on her daily strip of *Mug the Bug* at night. Otherwise, it was all housework and baking.

"Prudence?"

"Mm?"

"I've been meaning to ask you, you know the Scottish figurine the Hudsons found outside?"

"Mm."

"Where did Aunt Maggie usually keep it?"

"On her bedside table. I see you've got it in your studio."

"Yeah. Any ideas about how it got in the ground?"

"Nope. Doesn't make sense. It's too big for a cat to have dragged out and buried. You?"

Gerry sighed and wiped her sweaty forehead. "No, I don't, and it's bothering me." She resumed her task. "Does your Mrs. Smith have a way of looking into the past?"

Prudence sat back on her heels. They were washing the lower part of the walls in the living room. Small in comparison to the formal dining room, it still ran the whole width of the house. Twenty cats kicked up a lot of dirt and, as this was the room where the art show refreshments were to be laid out, they'd decided to give it a thorough clean. "You mean about Maggie's death and the cat?"

"Yeah." Gerry dipped her brush into the soapy water in the bucket and scrubbed, then reached for the cloth to wipe and dry.

"I could ask her next time I go," said Prudence.

"You sound doubtful."

"Well, we usually just sit and wait for Mother to begin. And I don't ask much, just tell her what I've been doing, the gossip."

"Actually, I saw a notice in the paper that Mrs. Smith will be at the tea room all week, telling fortunes. I thought I might go and see what she can tell me."

Prudence became defensive. "Well, I don't talk about you, just to say I work in the same house for the niece of the cousin I used to work for. I'd appreciate it if you wouldn't ask her about me."

Gerry was shocked. "Why would I do that? I respect your privacy. And Mrs. Smith wouldn't be so unethical as to discuss one client with another, would she?"

Prudence appeared mollified. "No. I suppose not. No. Of course she wouldn't. She'd lose all her trade."

"Does she have a lot of people who visit her regularly?" Gerry asked timidly, hoping she wasn't overstepping some boundary.

"Enough to support her." Prudence stood and inspected the walls. "They look good enough from up here. We better get cracking on the other rooms. The entranceway this afternoon, I think."

"All right. I'm just going to call the tea room and make an appointment."

Prudence had decreed that the cat boxes were due to be emptied and scrubbed and left in the sun to deodorize, so while she tackled that grim task, Gerry drove to the supermarket to buy ten big sacks of cat litter.

Margaret was shopping at the same time and sneered when she saw Gerry straining to push the heavily loaded cart to the cash. Gerry just nodded. She couldn't be bothered.

When she got home, there were the boxes, lined up in a row drying on the lawn. Bob and the boys were using them to play hide and seek, hopping in and out. Gerry took the opportunity to throw the plant Marigold had uprooted onto the compost pile behind the garage. She remembered it as one Aunt Mary had identified in her garden and resolved to look it up later.

She unpacked the cat litter, brought each sack onto the back porch and stacked it. "We'll be stacking wood here soon," said Prudence. "Most convenient location. Door leads to the centre of the house." When she saw Gerry's face, imagining her nice porch no longer available for sitting, she added, "But not till after Christmas. Till then it's not too bad going to the shed and bringing it through the kitchen, just messy."

The entranceway got washed and dusted and Prudence left, promising to come in early on Wednesday. Gerry remembered she'd promised to help Cathy with the snacks and phoned her. "I can give you tomorrow and maybe Friday a bit, but otherwise I'm busy."

Cathy thought out loud. "There's a lot we can do ahead of time. Come over tomorrow and we'll prep. Bring your cheese grater." Gerry promised to be there early and went off to try and crank out a couple of *Mug the Bug* strips. She worked until late in the evening.

When she arrived at Cathy's it was to find her friend had two enormous bowls prepared alongside a huge bag of flour and several giant wedges of cheese. "Get grating," Cathy said cheerfully. "We need the same amount of cheese as flour."

So they grated and grated and grated and grated, while Prince Charles salivated and kept watch for any bits of cheese that flew on the floor. "I probably shouldn't have him in here where we're working but if you don't mind, I don't mind."

"I don't mind. One dog compared to a houseful of cats is nothing."

The mound of cheese grew until it approximated the bagful of flour. "Good," said Cathy. "Now take half the flour and half the cheese in your bowl and I'll take the rest. Mix it. With your hands, girl," she exclaimed, as Gerry just stood there looking at the massive quantities. "We're cooking for a hundred people, remember?"

Gerry dug her hands in. At least it was dry. It wasn't unpleasant. After a while, Cathy said, "Okay. Now we work quickly because we don't want the butter to melt." She took about a dozen pounds of butter out of the fridge and gave half to Gerry along with a knife. "Chop into little cubes and throw into your bowl." When this was done, it was back in the bowl with bare hands.

Surprisingly, a heavy dough began to form. "That's it?" Gerry asked. "Don't you use recipes?"

"That's it. This *is* a recipe, given me by an old and dear friend. Now, cover with plastic film and chill. It needs a few hours, so before we move on, how about a break?"

Turned out, Cathy's idea of a break was to take Charles for a walk around her property and drink a quick coffee before getting back to work.

They cut the crusts off of at least twenty loaves of bread, buttered the slices and cut them in squares, triangles and fingers before storing them in giant plastic containers. "That's for the canapés," Cathy explained. "Can you chop these onions?"

Gerry blanched as Cathy slung a ten-pound sack onto the counter. She chopped and she chopped. Tears streamed down her cheeks. She found if she just left the tears and didn't blow her nose, it wasn't so bad. "This is disgusting!" she said. "I must look horrible." Charles whined and scratched to go out.

"I'm not looking," said Cathy, busy setting pots of eggs to boil on the stove. She released the dog. "Do you know the best way to make hard-boiled eggs?"

"I know a way. You boil the heck out of them."

"No. They only need five minutes, then put on the lids, turn off the heat and set your timer for twenty minutes. Soak in cold water for a while and they'll be easy to peel. Which, when you're doing six dozen at a time, is a good thing."

"I'm finished." Gerry took a roll of paper towel outside and tidied herself up. Charles looked sympathetically at her out of bloodshot eyes. "You know, don't you, Charles? You know."

When they returned to the kitchen, Gerry propped the door open. Cathy was frying the onions in many different pans. (The eggs were on the counter in their pots.) "I need your hands, Gerry."

"'Back into the valley of death, rode the six hundred,'" Gerry dramatically recited. "Or, words to that effect. Save yourself, Charles!" Charles flopped back down the kitchen steps outside, lay with his nose facing away from the kitchen.

"I need you to stir." Cathy handed Gerry two wooden spoons. "Keep the onions moving. You have four pans. I have four pans. It varies from ten minutes to half an hour, depending on the onions."

"Cathy, how do you do it?"

Cathy looked nonchalant. "Well, I don't cater for such large groups often. I'm more likely to cook a meal for from six to twenty guests, something like that. But I'm enjoying this. I like making party food. Besides, we're halfway done — for today."

"Do I get a break for lunch?" whined Gerry.

"Leftovers from the weekend. Roast beef and pickle sandwiches with sweet potato oven fries." Gerry made a happy little noise and stirred with a will.

The onions finally turned a warm golden brown, the eggs were peeled and stored, and lunch was eaten. Then they began to make the cheese straws.

Cathy demonstrated. "Tear off a good big lump like this. Whack it down onto a piece of waxed paper. Put another piece of paper on top and roll out till they're about this thick. Remove the top paper and cut the dough into roughly six-inch-long strips about an inch wide. It doesn't matter. We don't care if they're all exactly the same size. They just have to taste good."

She'd done her first lump of dough, start to finish, in about five minutes. Gerry's took twenty, with much sticky mishandling of the dough. Cathy watched this struggle, then couldn't stand it any longer. "I'll roll, you cut and twist. Right?" After that, things went much faster, and by the end of a few hours, they had two hundred cheese straws baked and cooling. Gerry was limp.

"I never realized cooking was so exhausting," she said, nibbling a cheese straw. "And you do this day after day?"

"Well, but it's varied. I'm never bored. If you can come in Friday morning, that would be great. We'll assemble the canapés and transport them over to your place."

That night, as she fell asleep, Gerry could have sworn her hands were still cutting and twisting hundreds and hundreds of cheese straws.

"Why," she moaned the next morning, "does everyone suddenly want me to bake?"

Prudence smiled sweetly. "We all want you to learn how to feed yourself, so you don't wind up living on coffee, cat meat and wine."

"Point taken."

"Besides, when you make something nice to eat and share it, you're giving a part of yourself — your time, your skill. People, good people, appreciate that."

"What are we making?"

"Hot milk cake."

"Hot milk cake."

"A cake made with hot milk in the batter. An old recipe."

"How old?"

"Well, my mother made it, so…old. Lots of beating involved but the good news is we have a mixer. It's a very simple recipe. I'm going to leave you and go check the cat boxes. See how far you can get."

Half an hour later, when Prudence returned, Gerry was carefully sliding a round cake tin into the hot oven. "It's just following instructions!" she said gleefully. "I can bake!"

Later Prudence showed her how to test the cake by first patting it gently, then inserting a toothpick into the centre to see if the batter was still at all gummy. If the toothpick was dry, it must be cake.

"We'll finish it just before the students come." As Gerry stood around, gloating over the smooth golden top of her cake, Prudence said, "You're dismissed. Class is finished," and Gerry left to prepare for the art component of the day.

After lunch, Prudence produced a bag of icing sugar, a small sieve and a paper doily. "You want to make sure it's completely cooled or the sugar will melt and become absorbed." Gerry the artist figured out what to do and gently decorated the cake.

As the class filed into the studio, they sniffed appreciatively. Cake was in the air.

Gerry was a believer that practice was one key to success in the arts, so she asked to see what they'd sketched from the first class and had them repeat that exercise, but this time with a time limit. She assured them it didn't matter if they didn't finish; it was just an exercise.

Then she asked them to choose one of the large objects in the room — a piece of furniture, the fireplace, a window — and draw that. "From micro to macro. We learn to focus in different ways, depending on the subject and our intention." A gentle tap on the door rescued the students and Gerry from any more philosophizing on art, and not a moment too soon. Only Christine looked interested; the rest were starting to get a glazed look in their eyes. They were far more interested in cake.

"Teaching is hard," said Gerry to Prudence as they tidied up the dishes.

"It's work. It's supposed to be hard."

"Anyway, they're all coming to the vernissage, so that's five for sure, eight with you, me and Cathy."

"I wouldn't worry. Free wine and food? You'll be mobbed."

After a night spent tossing through dreams of running out of refreshments and guests getting really, really angry with her, Gerry woke to a rainy morning. She felt tense and had to calm herself, saying, "You can do this. Just prioritize." She began to assemble and hang the components of her exhibition. Mr. Shipton dropped off their garden painting, then Gerry walked to Cathy's and to Mr. Parminter's to collect their house paintings. She had room in between them to hang a few of her miniatures of flowers. Then she went around the house and assembled Aunt Maggie's efforts and arranged and hung them. Finally, she took the other miscellaneous paintings and put them up in the gallery.

By two o'clock she was done, changed and headed to her first fortune-telling experience.

The Two Sisters' Tea Room was on the main drag of Lovering. One large room, it was usually only half full but today was packed.

One table with two chairs had been moved to a back corner and it was there that Gerry supposed the medium sat. She was with a customer who appeared to be breaking down in tears, wiping her face, hiding it with her hands.

Other customers besides Gerry cast furtive glances. She didn't want to stare, so looked around the room. Shelves lined half the walls: teacups, teapots, cream and sugar sets and many tea varieties in tins made for a colourful display. The other walls held examples of local artists' work. Gerry got up and had a look. Maybe she could —

"You have to pick out your cup."

Gerry jumped. "What?"

The inevitable teenage girl repeated, "You pick out the cup you want. Over there." She gestured at a tall set of open shelves. Gerry walked over and, without really thinking too much about it, chose a white china cup and saucer with a broad crimson band running around the top of the cup and outer edge of the saucer. A thin gold trim completed the lush effect. She returned with the cup to her table. The girl returned too. "What kinda tea?"

"Do you have Earl Grey? I'll have a pot of that. Oh, and a scone with everything."

The weeping customer left and another edged over to the table. Sheesh, thought Gerry. I hope this one doesn't go to pieces.

The teenager reappeared with the tea and scone. "You getting your fortune told?"

"Yes. At three o'clock."

"Don't strain the tea."

"What?"

The girl rolled her eyes. "Don't strain the tea. Pour it. Drink it. Then leave the leaves in your cup. She reads them."

"I see. Thanks." Gerry did as instructed as she wolfed down the scone with butter, clotted cream and strawberry jam. She'd not had time for lunch. Her tea leaves formed an unsightly clump at the bottom of the cup. The previous customer left and went back to her friends at her table. It was three o'clock, so Gerry approached, bearing her cup. "Mrs. Smith?"

The woman was about sixty, plain, with thin light brown hair pulled back in a skinny bun. She was the opposite of exotic, and Gerry found this reassuring. Mrs. Smith smiled and nodded and looked in Gerry's cup.

She asked Gerry to pour a little tea from the teapot on Mrs. Smith's table into her cup, swirl the contents, then spill the excess liquid into her saucer. Now that there were leaves splayed on the inside of the cup's side, she could begin.

"You are generous. You are kind. You have known some sadness but not too much. You are resilient. You are trying to ignore some signs, some warnings."

Gerry tried to maintain a poker face so Mrs. Smith wouldn't know if she'd hit a sensitive area with her remarks, but Mrs. Smith just seemed to be looking at the tea leaves. "Three, no four signs — the fourth one will be repeated — but you don't want to think about them. The first and fourth signs should combine to open your eyes. Do you have any questions?"

Gerry thought for a moment. "Will I make enough money to support my — family?"

Mrs. Smith smiled. "You will always work hard and always have enough."

"Will I have a husband, children?"

Mrs. Smith nodded. "But not right away."

That suited Gerry. She wasn't ready to settle down. But she got a warm feeling, thinking of the future. Mrs. Smith continued. "There are shadows, but beyond these, a darker one." She waved her hand in front of her face. "Someone is trying — I can't see — no, it's gone." She straightened up. "Pay the girl, please."

Gerry rose. "Thank you," she said politely. She strolled out into the afternoon drizzle, her mind roiling. What signs? What in recent memory struck her as a "sign"? She wasn't someone given to noticing such portents. And then, given what she'd just been sipping, it struck her: *teacups!* Twice Marigold had tipped a teacup. Then what might be the third? The figurine buried in the garden? If those were three, then what was the fourth? And it was about to be repeated. She looked at the time, squealed and headed for home.

Doug had been and gone, had rigged up three of his "objects" on rocks by the shore. A long thick extension cord connected them to the house's outside outlet. A timer prevented Gerry from checking the effect.

She fed the cats. She put up the explicatory cards on the walls of the gallery, found a few typos and stomped upstairs to retype those cards. She got distracted by what she was going to wear and spent an hour pulling clothes out of the cupboard and trying them on, much to the delight of Bob, who pounced on every discarded garment. She decided on two alternatives and laid those clothes aside. She got hungry. She ordered a pizza. She ate the pizza. She paced from room to room, fretting about the parking, the cats, the food. She phoned Cathy. No answer. She dashed next door to see Mr. Parminter but got no reply when she knocked on the back door or went around to ring at the front one.

She went home. She looked for Lightning and gave her an extra feed and some attention, which still just meant chatting to the beast while it crouched in a corner, vibrating with negative energy.

She searched for Marigold and finally found her asleep on Aunt Maggie's bed. She tried a long hot bath and fell asleep in it, only to wake an hour later feeling completely refreshed. She clumped downstairs into her studio and finished the portrait of Mitzi — three months early! She became inspired and made herself laugh designing a label for Cathy's catering company. Stribling's Fine Foods with By Appointment to Prince Charles underneath — and with a coat of arms that featured sausage rolls, cheese straws and a pair of bassets, rampant.

Whatever that means, she thought. She hoped it meant on their hind legs, because that's what she'd drawn. Something else I have to look up. What was the other thing? She couldn't remember, yawned, and finally went to sleep.

12

Prudence must have come in extra, extra early, because when Gerry woke up it was nine o'clock and Bob and Marigold were both gone. She sat up with a jerk. Prioritize, her brain screamed. Get a move on, a calmer voice urged. Right. I can do this. I have until seven tonight. I have until seven. Right. Right. Gotta go to Cathy's. Okay.

Shouting, "Bye, Prudence," in the direction of the kitchen, she jumped in her car and drove to Cathy's. She raced to the kitchen door and surprised a sleepy-looking Cathy, sitting in bathrobe and slippers at the table. "I'm here!" she said dramatically and fell into the room. Charles gave her a sorrowful stare, then subsided onto his side with a long, shuddering sigh.

"Coffee?" Cathy offered.

"Um, okay. Aren't we in a hurry?"

"I couldn't sleep so did the chicken livers in the middle of the night. I can handle the rest, dear. I just need you to take some trays and the cheese straws."

By ten, Gerry had delivered the snacks that were ready to her own kitchen and was stacking them in the fridge. "What are you doing here?" Prudence had her arms full of cat towels for the laundry. "I thought you'd be hours."

"I know. Cathy has it so under control, she just wants me to go back after lunch for another load of trays, then she'll bring the rest at six and start putting on the finishing touches."

"You could go get the wine," Prudence suggested.

"The wine! Right!" Gerry drove to Lovering's tiny liquor store and picked up her order. Is there anything else I need while I'm in town? she wondered. "Paper napkins! Plastic cups!" she said aloud.

The guy in the liquor store suggested the grocery store probably had those, so she drove there and made her purchases. When she got back in the car, she looked at its clock: only ten thirty. She drove home and unloaded her purchases.

"The red wine goes here on the table and the white wine goes in the fridge, of course." Prudence was laying a white cloth on the living room's long table.

"We're out of room in the fridge!" Gerry exclaimed hysterically. "No room for the wine!"

"Nonsense," said Prudence. "I'll make room. You arrange the cups and napkins on the table. Then I need you to go for a walk."

"Go for a walk," Gerry repeated.

"Yes. Settle down. Go up into the woods. Wear your rubber boots. It'll be wet."

Gerry was putting on her boots when she heard the by-now-familiar "beep, beep, beep, beep." "Oh, no. Oh, no, no, no, no!" she said as she ran into the road.

Sure enough, the Hudsons had chosen the day of her art show to replace the damaged fence. She walked slowly over to them, trying not to hyperventilate. "Hi," she managed to say casually. "How long do you think it'll take?"

The older giant spoke. "Couple of hours now. Lunch. 'Nother hour. Two, two-thirty."

"I see," she said in her best lady-of-the-manor voice. "Thank you so much." And escaped.

It was a beautiful day but it took Gerry some time to notice it. She crossed the road and followed the grass and dirt lane that divided Andrew's cottage from Cathy's spacious lawns, up past the cow pastures and into the woods. After she crossed the train tracks, the forest became older, full of mature trees that darkened and cooled the path. She stopped at the old sugar shack.

Somebody must still run sap from the giant maples into the shack, for the plastic lines were up and looked well maintained. There was a padlock on the crooked little front door, but Gerry knew, if she wanted to, she could easily get in by a back or side window. She'd done it often enough when she was a child let loose in the woods on vacations.

A scuffle among last year's dead leaves made her turn. "Uncle Geoff! What are you doing up here?"

He held up first the gun and then the birds that dangled from his other hand. "Partridge. Good to eat. You should wear a red hat when you go into the woods. Don't want to get shot."

He seemed like a different man when he was away from his wife and home: calm, peaceful. They fell into step.

"Did you walk all the way here from your house?" asked Gerry.

"Naw. Got my car parked in the development, where the tracks cross the road, that way." He pointed and the birds swung in the air.

"Prudence sent me out of the house. I guess I was getting on her nerves. Tonight is my art exhibit vernissage. Are you coming?"

"Ah, probably not, Gerry. No offense, but it's just not my thing. I heard Margaret and Mary talking about it though." He smiled. "I wish you luck."

"Thanks, Uncle Geoff." They'd returned to the tracks. He headed left and Gerry kept straight. It had been a good idea to walk. She felt steadier, ready for the rest of the day.

The opening night of her show was a blast. Gerry wore her little black dress and one of Aunt Maggie's retro fringed shawls: red roses, green leaves on cream. All her students came and brought their friends or family. The Parsleys were out in full force, not just Judy's immediate relations, but the Parsley Inn Parsleys, who came partly to see the art, but also to keep an eye on two of their offspring Gerry had hired as servers. She wanted Prudence to be a guest.

Prudence arrived wearing a rather splendid emerald green dress, with black shoes and purse, and a pearl necklace.

Cathy worked hard, heating snacks and sending them out of the kitchen, while Gerry greeted people in the foyer, then directed them into the gallery. After they emerged from there, they were sent on into the living room for their wine. After that, they were free to meander from room to room as they pleased.

Bea and Cece arrived. It was a walking day for Bea, but Gerry noticed she quickly found a chair where Cece brought her refreshments. Gerry was glad to see how people gravitated to their corner of the living room.

Before long the house was packed and people were talking their heads off. "There must be about seventy-five people here." Gerry squeezed Prudence's arm in excitement. "And the cats are no bother."

In truth, most of the cats, put off by the noise in their formal dining room, soon vacated it for upstairs or outside (where they sniffed the new fence), and Prudence was able to whisk cat towels off of available chairs before anyone haired up their good clothes.

Only the boys were overcome with excitement and chased each other up the dining room curtains, from where they were detached one by one by a sweating Gerry and deposited outside. She blocked the cat flap with a large urn, and resumed being elegant.

Right on cue, shortly after sunset, she began to hear exclamations from people looking out of the back windows. Doug's neon installations were creating a beautiful effect as they blinked and cascaded cool colours — green, blue, aqua, white — that reflected on the lake. Some people took their drinks onto the lawn to get a better look. Gerry found Doug and gave him a thumbs-up from across the room.

Andrew was there, and David. No sign of David's brothers. And it wasn't until after eight-thirty that Mary and Margaret arrived. As he'd vowed, Uncle Geoff was absent.

Mary handed her wrap to Prudence but Gerry quickly took it, saying, "Prudence is my guest tonight, Aunt Mary."

Mary sniffed and moved on, stuck her head in the gallery and remarked, "Very nice," in a quiet voice, then added, much more loudly, "Where are the refreshments?" and went off in search of them.

Margaret took her time in the gallery, pausing before each object, slowing down when she got to the fourth wall displaying the works collected by the Coneybears over almost two centuries. When she left the room, she seemed angry, but smug. With Margaret it was difficult to tell, so Gerry politely indicated where she might go to get a drink.

Marigold hopped slowly down the stairs from the bedrooms and sat in the foyer. Most of the other guests had left, taking note of the seven-to-nine timing of the event, but Gerry's family members were gathered there, finishing their drinks.

Marigold visited Gerry, who was reading comments and names in the guest book she'd placed by the door. Marigold sniffed her legs, pressed briefly against them and moved on.

She sniffed Doug and then David with a little more attention. David bent down to pet her. She sat by Andrew's feet, looking up into his face for a long time. Gerry saw Andrew shift his feet and look down nervously at the little cat. Finally, she moved away to sniff at Margaret's slim brown shoes. Margaret kicked out. "Get it away," she hissed at Gerry, but Marigold had already moved on to Aunt Mary, sniffed her legs and feet and sat down. Mary looked like she couldn't have cared less. Gerry could tell that her aunt, after a few glasses of wine and some delicious high-calorie snacks, was feeling pretty pleased with herself. If she'd been a cat, she'd have been purring.

Someone must have left a door open, because Bob appeared, dragging a withered object. He dropped it on the ground between Margaret and Mary, then rolled on his back, wriggling with glee. Margaret screamed, "Get that filthy thing away from me." Everyone looked but only Gerry moved. She picked the object up and patted Bob. He had retrieved Marigold's dug-up dead plant from the compost.

Mary laughed. "Has he brought us some catnip? Is that your cat's stash, Gerry?"

"What is it?" Gerry asked, raising the plant so all could see it.

"Monkshood," said Mary. "Aconite."

Someone sharply and suddenly caught their breath. Gerry thought it had been Prudence.

"Why are we all standing around and staring at an old plant the cat dragged in?" Margaret complained. "Mother, come. I'll take you home."

Mary cackled. "Thank you, Gerry. Always nice to revisit the ancestral home."

Gerry, having no trouble holding back what should have been a gracious invitation to drop in again, coldly bid her aunt and cousin good night.

The men left next. Andrew looked troubled. Prudence was last and clasped Gerry's shoulders as they paused at the door. "Be careful, dear. Something is not right." And Gerry could only nod and kiss her cheek.

Gerry sat on the stairs, her elbows on her knees, her chin in her cupped hands. "The fourth sign will be repeated." Two tipped teacups, one china lady, one dead plant. And then, "The first and fourth signs should combine to open your eyes." Marigold tipping Aunt Maggie's teacup and the dug-up plant were related?

All the elation of the successful evening left her and she went tiredly up to bed.

Saturday and Sunday afternoons between one and four, she was open for visitors, but only got a few. Cathy sent that weekend's paying guests over for a look; a few tourists passing pulled in briefly.

Gerry made cups of tea and chatted with these people, but the days were a bit anti-climactic after Friday night. Outside of the visiting hours, she flumped around the house in sweats or pyjamas, feeding the cats, trying to understand what it all meant.

Aunt Maggie had died. She'd had a heart condition and her doctor was satisfied that was the cause of death — heart failure.

Prudence had found her body. Prudence had washed out a teacup after Marigold knocked it over. Sign number one — only nobody knew it.

Marigold had knocked over another dangerous teacup. The wasp might have stung Prudence inside her throat and that could have killed her. Sign number two — and Prudence began to think, told Gerry about the first cup. That had gotten Gerry thinking.

A porcelain figurine was found intact, but buried at the side of the house. A gift from Andrew to Aunt Maggie, yet he'd seemed unconcerned when Gerry queried him about it. Sign number three didn't seem to make much sense to Gerry, seemed to be unconnected to the other signs.

Ah, yes, sign number four. One cat digs up a poisonous plant and, when this is ignored by the humans, another cat drags said plant into the middle of a party and leaves it near two of the dead woman's closest relations — her sister and her niece. One of her nieces. Gerry being the other one.

Wait, wait. I'm missing something, she thought. Oh yeah, I was going to look up that plant.

There was a row of gardening books on a shelf in the living room. She grabbed a couple of the larger encyclopaedic ones and sat in a rocker by the hearth.

Sunday's sun seemed quick to set — it was dark at only seven-thirty — and she shivered. Soon she'd be heating this big old house. She pictured a fire in the huge fireplace at her feet. She also pictured Aunt Maggie sitting where she was sitting, a cat in her lap. It wasn't fair if she'd been hurried on out of her life before her proper time.

She opened the first book, a British one, and found a colour photograph of *Aconitum napellus*. It showed a clump of delicate leaves and several spikes of bright blue flowers. It could have been similar to the plants in her garden but the plants had been photographed from too far away to make identification a sure thing.

She opened another book. This one was without colour photos for the most part, used pen and ink drawings. These were more helpful: close up and detailed. Aconite was the first herb in the book. She looked from the withered plant on the floor to the drawing in the book. It could be.

The text read: ACONITE (*Aconitum napellus*): A perennial to three feet tall, with deep green, finely divided leaves and dark blue hooded flowers in large spikes in July and August. The rhizomes have been used as a sedative, painkiller, and to treat rheumatism. All parts are poisonous.

She had a thought, got a flashlight, and slipped into the garden, trying to remember where Marigold had dug up the plant. She crouched next to the remaining clump and let the light play over the leaves.

Got it! There were the "finely divided leaves," the few remaining "hooded" flowers. They looked more like helmets than monks' hoods to her.

She stood up, thinking. Rhizomes? What the heck were they? She went back into the house, looked it up in Aunt Maggie's plant book. Basically, lumpy roots as opposed to hairlike ones. She held up Marigold's specimen. Yup. Lumpy roots.

But surely, when Maggie died in May, the plant would have been a low mound of green. So that meant, if that was how she'd been killed, someone had to be a real plant expert to recognize it. Gerry knew she'd have trouble recognizing even a rose bush if it wasn't in bloom. Aunt Mary had said the sisters had a lot of the same plants in their gardens and had boasted that she was an expert.

"More research is required," Gerry told Bob, who was sitting on the padded bench that ran along one of the short walls under the bookshelf. "You seem to be okay. I guess touching the leaves of the plant with your mouth isn't dangerous.

"So, wait. If Aunt Maggie drank aconite tea, wouldn't it have shown in any tests done after her death? Or does heart disease mean they wouldn't have bothered with tests for poison? Yes. Why would they? So, assume no tests like that were done and she's been cremated, so there's no point in me involving any authorities like the hospital, the police.

"I don't know, Bob. What should I do?" Bob sat up, yawned and recurled himself into a warm ball of fur. Gerry took the hint and went to bed.

When Prudence arrived Monday morning, Gerry was making aconite tea.

13

"Are you crazy?" Prudence exclaimed. "All these dishes and the counters will have to be scrubbed after you're done. No, sterilized. What if you poison the cats?"

"Mm?" Gerry looked up from where she was grating fresh aconite roots onto a piece of the *Lovering Herald*. She was wearing gloves and an apron. "Don't worry, I've already fed them. We'll just do an extra good clean of the kitchen when we're finished."

"I'd say we'll need to," Prudence remarked more calmly, noting the mud tracked in by the boots Gerry was still wearing, the decapitated plants on the floor, the bits of grated root flying around the room. "I suppose it's good practice. I thought we could make carrot cake for the students this week." When Gerry looked blank, she added, "Carrots. You have to grate carrots."

Gerry giggled. "Oh, I thought you were suggesting we put aconite in the cake and finish them all off."

Prudence examined her. "Are you okay? You look a bit funny."

"Prudence, I have worked it out that my aunt was murdered by someone she trusted enough to bring her a cup of tea in her bedroom. That can only be you or someone from the rest of my family. How do you expect I should look?"

"Well, I didn't do it."

"I never said you did." Gerry raised her gloved hands, adding grimly, "Kettle's boiling. Let's make tea."

They waited a good ten minutes, then poured the liquid into a cup. "Does that look the same colour as the stuff in Aunt Maggie's cup?" Gerry whispered. "And why am I whispering?"

Prudence whispered back, "Because this is dreadful. It's so easy. To kill someone with a common garden plant." She tipped some of the liquid into the cup's saucer. "It looks the same." She straightened and spoke in her normal tone. "But you realize it looks the same as any herb tea — kind of weak and yellowy. What have we proved?"

"That it's easy to do, as you said. That the plant could be harvested with or without flowers present if you know your plants."

"We're still guessing all this, Gerry. Surely, they would have tested the contents of her stomach."

"I don't know. Maybe that's only done on TV. It's probably too expensive to do on everyone. And with the doctor right there, blabbing about her heart…"

There was a pause as they thought. "Well, what do you propose to do next?"

Gerry smiled. "A bit of sleuthing."

"Not alone, you're not. That's what the amateur sleuth always does on TV and then of course the murderer has a chance to kill them too."

"All right. I'll set things up and you can come with me."

Prudence looked taken aback. "Me? What about Doug or Andrew, someone big and strong?"

"You're big and strong and they're suspects."

"Really?"

"Sure. Andrew especially. He lives just there." They both glanced nervously through the kitchen window at Andrew's cottage. It had been a cool night and a lake mist was drifting through his garden, obscuring the lower half of the house. They shivered, then started, as Andrew, whistling, came out the front door and drove off to work.

Gerry cleared her throat. "He lives just there. He was second on the spot after you found Aunt Maggie's body. Was he ever alone with her?"

Prudence thought. "I called him and he came through the front door and ran up the stairs. I waited in the hall, so, yes, he was alone, just for a couple of minutes."

"Long enough to alter evidence!" Gerry concluded triumphantly.

"But what would he have to alter, if he did it? He had all night. And the teacup was still there when I cleaned the room later."

Gerry's face fell. "Oh. You're right. This is harder than I thought. Okay, well, Doug then. He could have paddled over in the middle of the night, let himself in — "

"Made tea and presented her with it?" Prudence finished the faltering Gerry's sentence sarcastically. "And what's his motive? Why would Doug kill Maggie?"

"You've got me there." Gerry tried to take off the rubber gloves. Her hands had sweated and they stuck. She went to put one finger in her mouth to pull them off when Prudence lunged at her with a cry.

"You'll poison yourself! You do need a minder. Right. You do nothing without me. Got it?" She gingerly peeled the gloves off of Gerry inside out and threw them in the garbage. "I'll clean this up. You go and paint something."

"Yes, Prudence. Anything you say, Prudence." A chastened and somewhat trembly Gerry went into her studio and sat facing the fireplace. The Scottish lady gleamed dully on the mantel. Marigold entered the room and tried to hop onto Gerry's lap, couldn't make it and fell. Gerry tenderly picked her up. "You started all this, Marigold, but I know you're just a little cat. I don't expect you to finish it."

Gerry looked at the figurine. Was it an important clue? Mrs. Smith hadn't mentioned it when she spoke about signs.

Doug and Andrew didn't seem like very strong suspects, especially Doug. Even if Margaret inherited Aunt Gerry's house, she and Doug were a divorced couple. He wouldn't get anything. "That's it!" She sat upright, waking the cat. "Prudence! Prudence!"

Prudence came running, wiping her hands on a tea towel. "Whatever is it now?" she exclaimed.

"It's not about the house and Aunt Maggie's stuff. Because no one knew who inherited. Am I right?" Prudence nodded. "So why kill someone when there was only a chance you might inherit? She might have left it all to the cats for all the potential heirs knew."

"Yee-es." Prudence sat down next to Gerry, reached out and petted the cat.

"So. Don't you see? Financial gain couldn't have been the motive. Something else got Aunt Maggie poisoned. An emotion, like rage or jealousy. Aunt Mary seems to have always been jealous of Aunt Maggie."

Prudence nodded again. "Which I thought was strange, as it was Mary who married a wonderful man who'd do anything for her, had children. Whereas Maggie had an old house full of cats."

"Ah, but Maggie was loved. By her cats, by you, by her neighbours. Mary knew that. And she must know there aren't very many people who love her."

"Geoff, Andrew and Margaret. I don't think her grandsons like her very much. And Maggie loved her sister, though she found her difficult."

"Who else was jealous of Maggie? Andrew? Nah. He likes his work, his china, his house. Margaret? Maybe. But surely she'll inherit from her parents?"

Prudence spoke slowly. "But they're not really old yet. What if Margaret didn't want to wait? Who would inherit if Maggie was dead? Margaret must have thought her mother. We all did. Maybe Mary idly said, 'When I inherit Maggie's place, you can have it' to Margaret."

"So we're back to the house being the motive," Gerry concluded glumly.

"Gerry."

"Yes?"

"Who inherits if you die?"

"Well, I don't have a will yet, or any children, so—" They looked at each other and their eyes widened. "It would go to Mary as Maggie's last surviving sibling. Oh, Prudence!"

Prudence looked worried. "We better sort this mess out quickly. Until we do, you may be in danger."

There was a lot of tidying and cleaning and rearranging of furniture to do inside and out after the busy weekend. Prudence worked in the house while Gerry wandered around outside, picking up cigarette butts and the odd plastic cup or napkin.

The mist had soaked the lawn, though by mid-morning, most of the thickest patches had dissipated, leaving thin wisps to streak the surface of the lake.

The cats didn't like it, stayed on the flagstone paths where they could keep their feet dry. Only Marigold followed Gerry about, herself a thin wisp of a cat, her ribs showing through her scant coat.

Gerry had seen photos of Marigold in her prime. What a pretty cat she had been—fluffy, dainty, her tricolour coat unique, as all calicoes are. Now her disease had matted and clumped the once wonderful fur. On skinny legs, she walked ahead of Gerry, to the spot where the rest of the aconite plants flourished, sat and looked up at her. "All right. I'll start there," Gerry promised.

After a sober lunch, Gerry and Prudence drove to Mary and Geoff's. "We'll start with the queen and then go tackle the princess," Gerry quipped.

But the princess was there. Margaret answered the door, her mother behind her, curious who it might be. Though they were alone together, both Mary and Margaret wore make up, their hair had been done and they wore skirts with matching sweaters and high heels. Gerry contrasted her sweats and Prudence's plain blouse and slacks. "Are you expecting company?" she asked Mary.

"No, but come in anyway," Mary invited dryly. She gestured to the interior. They walked through to the kitchen where they saw the ladies were in the middle of their lunch. "What do you want?" Mary asked rudely, sitting back down and picking up her knife and fork.

Gerry and Prudence sat on the couch in the living space that was down a few steps and adjacent to the kitchen. Margaret stared at them. "Eat your lunch, Margaret," Mary ordered. Margaret picked at her food nervously.

"We came to ask you — " Gerry's voice came out high-pitched and shaky. She stopped and collected herself. "We want to know if you had anything to do with Aunt Maggie's death."

Aunt Mary became very still for a moment. Then Margaret choked. "Got a bit of quiche stuck," she said hoarsely, then proceeded to cough for a few minutes, before she could drink some water. "That's better."

Gerry waited. Mary spoke first. "What have you heard?" She drank from her wine glass, gestured to Margaret to refill it from the bottle on the table.

"I haven't — we haven't heard anything. But I've noticed a lot of weird things at the house. Prudence has too." Gerry didn't want to be specific. After all, the clues, except the china figurine, were all cat-related. How would that sound? My aunt's cat is indicating someone poisoned her.

At mention of Prudence, Mary sneered. "Prudence! And how is the faithful retainer this morning?"

"What's a retainer?" Margaret sounded puzzled. "David has one for his teeth."

"You're an idiot, Margaret." Tears welled in Margaret's eyes. "Retainer is an old word for servant, which you'd know if you ever read anything other than décor mags."

"Andrew reads décor mags," said Gerry, drawn to defend Margaret, though unwillingly. "So do I. I quite like them."

"Andrew presumably reads them for work and you're an artist, but Margaret's just a foolish housewife who barely made it out of high school before she got herself pregnant."

"I'm fine, Cousin. Thanks for asking." Prudence's voice cut into the conversation like a sabre taking an arm off an opponent. "And Margaret struggled in school because you alternately praised and criticized her so the poor girl didn't know whether she was a genius or a fool."

Mary was silenced, pushed her plate away and leaned back, toying with the stem of her wineglass, rolling it between her fingers.

Gerry thought it was time to get back on track. "We, Prudence and I, have reason to believe that Aunt Maggie was poisoned by a cup of herbal tea prepared from a plant common to both her and your gardens." She paused and looked at Margaret. "Do you have a garden?"

"Don't be stupid." Mary spoke for her daughter, who was sitting with her mouth open. "How could she afford a gardener? The boys cut the grass and that's it." She looked interested as she added, "What plant, specifically?"

Gerry took a deep breath. "Aconite. Monkshood."

"Well, I don't know how you'd die, but it's certainly supposed to be poisonous." Mary looked curiously at Gerry. "And you really think one of us would do that?"

"Who else would Aunt Maggie let into her house, much less her bedroom, than a family member?" There was a strange quietness in the room after Gerry spoke. The four women all looked at each other. Gerry broke the silence. "I was in Toronto."

"I was at home alone," said Prudence.

"I was with you, Mother, until about ten that evening, then I went home. The boys were there when I arrived."

"And I was obviously here and Geoff would have been somewhere about, working in the basement on something or other, or watching TV."

Gerry spoke slowly. "So none of you really has an alibi, as you, Margaret, could have driven to Aunt Maggie's on your way home, and you, Aunt Mary, could have slipped out after Margaret left."

"And what about Prudence?"

"Why would Prudence kill Maggie?" Gerry watched her aunt and cousin closely.

Margaret spoke. "Maybe Maggie told Prudence about her ridiculous will and Prudence needed the ten thousand dollars."

"For what?" an exasperated Gerry demanded.

Mary snorted with laughter. "Maybe to pay that creepy Mrs. Smith for séances, hmm, Prudence? So you can 'talk' to your mother. My Aunt Constance. Boy, there was a whacko. And Prudence has inherited her craziness, by the looks of it. The Parsleys always did have a mongrel streak. Why, look who Prudence chose to marry?"

"Enough!" thundered Prudence, rising. "Gerry, we're finished here."

A dumbstruck Gerry followed Prudence out to the car. "Prudence, what on earth?"

"Just drive, Gerry," Prudence said through gritted teeth. "Just drive."

When they got near The Maples, Gerry broke the silence. "Do you want to get the carriage?"

Prudence replied angrily, "No. I know you think it makes me look foolish. Just take me home."

"I don't know where you live," Gerry said gently.

"I'll tell you when to stop."

When they got to Station Road, Prudence gestured to turn. Gerry turned. They went up the first little hill, around the big curve and over the tracks. Station Road was traditionally where some of the less affluent members of Lovering society lived. Some of the houses were in stages of refurbishment, exhibiting tarps over unfinished roofs and scaffolding where partly torn-apart walls might linger for years. Yet people lived in them. Other houses were better kept, and it was to one of these, a little white cottage, that Prudence directed Gerry.

"Why Prudence, it's lovely!" And it was.

A one-storey building, it sported a tiny peaked front roof with delicate white cut-out detail, pale blue tiles and similarly coloured shutters and window boxes. These were filled with salmon-pink geraniums and trailing white lobelia. The whole was sparkling white, freshly painted. "It's like a little jewel!" exclaimed Gerry.

"It's not bad," grudgingly admitted Prudence. "Thank you for the ride." She got out of the car.

"See you Wednesday," Gerry called, then thought, I hope I see you on Wednesday. Worried that the ugly afternoon might have affected her relationship with Prudence, Gerry sadly drove home.

She stopped at Cathy's to pay her for the catering, but her friend wasn't there, so she drove home and fed the cats. She fixed herself a plate of leftovers and sat at the table in the living room looking out at the lake. The cats knew better than to beg from her while she was eating, but that didn't stop some of them from sitting under the table hoping for crumbs. It was nice to know their warm, furry bodies were nearby. She felt closest to her aunt in this room. "She must have sat here plenty of times, eh, guys?"

She heard a car drive up. Someone opened the door and stood on the kitchen porch, rattling the kitchen doorknob. "Gerry, it's me. It's Margaret." Gerry sat very still. Then she heard a key turn in the lock and Margaret was in the kitchen. She looked into the room where Gerry sat among the cats. "Why Gerry, that's where Aunt Maggie used to sit."

Gerry's mouth hung open. "A key. You have a key. And you just used it to let yourself into my house."

Margaret looked down at her hand. "Oh, this is Mother's. I borrowed it. I have to talk to you."

"First, I need that key, Margaret." She wondered how many other copies were floating around. Did Andrew have one?

Margaret put the key on the table and sat down in one of the dining chairs next to Gerry. "I remember when I was little coming here with Mother and Andrew. And Dad. Of course, you weren't born yet. Gramma Ellie was still here. I vaguely remember Grampa Matthew but he died when I was very young."

Despite her caution around her cousin, Gerry was interested. Here was Margaret, chatting about Gerry's grandparents, her father's parents, who she'd never had the chance of knowing. "What were they like?"

"Grampa was tall and heavy. He was a banker or something. Something in the city. He took the train every day. That's where they found him, slumped in his seat on the train one afternoon. Missed his stop, and the conductor in those days knew where everybody should be getting off, so he shook his shoulder but he was dead." She stopped talking abruptly.

"And Gramma Ellie?" Gerry prompted gently.

"Oh, I liked her. She'd been brought up strict and went the other way, spoiled her children and grandchildren. She would have us over and cook special things. Little cakes just for us children. Pink icing for me. Blue for Andrew." Margaret paused again, stuck in some memory she seemed loath to leave.

"Aunt Maggie lived here too, right?"

"Yes. But no one paid much attention to her. She was five years younger than my mother, but it seemed the other way, as if she was older. She was always going off somewhere to read or draw, or nurse a sick cat." Margaret drew her feet together under her chair. "I don't like them, you know."

"I can tell."

"It's their eyes. So cold. Not like dog eyes. I like dogs."

"Did you know my father at all? When he was young?"

"No. He was already gone. Then first Grampa and then Gramma died and in the will it said the house went to Maggie. Mummy was terribly angry. She screamed and screamed. Daddy kept telling her to be quiet but she slapped him. I heard it. It got very quiet in the house. He went out. Mummy cried for hours."

Gerry felt creeped out that Margaret had dropped her usual formal appellation of "Mother" for the infantile "Mummy," but supposed if Margaret was regressing to describe a childhood experience, it might be normal.

Margaret continued in a harder voice. "Then I married Doug. I was pregnant — only just — with James, and Mother and Dad insisted. At first it was nice, having a house and a baby. But then I had the others close together and the house was too small, Doug started drinking and struggled with going to work.

"Do you know what it's like living with an alcoholic?"

Gerry shook her head.

"It takes a while before you realize. And he was perfectly nice, as long as he had his twelve beers a day. Beer for breakfast, beer for lunch, beer for supper. Beer until he'd pass out in front of the TV in the middle of the night, spill the dregs on his clothes or the furniture.

"Do you know what it's like being terrified to sleep because you're afraid your husband is going to set himself and you and your house of babies on fire from his cigarettes? I'd find them burned out on the floor around his easy chair where he'd dropped them."

Margaret was shaking with anger and, despite her dislike for her cousin, Gerry felt sorry for the woman. She'd certainly been unlucky. "You had a bad time," she said gently.

Margaret's head snapped back. "I don't need your sympathy, Gerry. You being nice to Doug! How do you think that makes me feel? I'm your cousin, not him."

Gerry began explaining. "Well, actually, he's kind of both our cousins — "

But Margaret interrupted. "Anyway, that's not why I'm here." Her face took on a look of cunning as she leaned forward. "Earlier you said you think Aunt Maggie was poisoned by some herb or something? Well, I heard Mother, before Aunt Maggie died, recommending an herbal tea to her, for insomnia. She said she took it herself, which is a laugh. The only thing Mother takes when she can't sleep is a large brandy."

"You're accusing your mother?" Gerry asked incredulously.

Margaret rose to leave. "I just thought you should know. Ask her yourself." Predictably, she slammed both the kitchen and porch doors.

Oh, I will, thought Gerry, as she wearily locked up and went to bed.

14

Tuesday Gerry took a break from it all, drove to the train station and treated herself to a day at the museum.

She had to confess a preference for the modern art over the old masters, though she spent a lot of time looking at the Impressionists, who, in her opinion, linked the other two categories.

She remembered one of her teachers at art college suggested that, as artists, they always ask, "What can I learn from this?" And it was in that spirit that she toured the various galleries within the museum.

Though she'd never constructed one, she was fascinated by the installations, art as experience, three-dimensional, surrounding the patron with not just visual but aural, sometimes tactile sensations.

If you can imagine it and make it, it's art, she thought, as she moved dreamily from artist to artist.

She bypassed the small, trendy bistro on the building's top floor for a late lunch in the cafeteria, where its less affluent customers unselfconsciously ate sandwiches and drank milk or soda, then she visited the Canadian section.

There'd been a real flowering in Canadian painting in the early twentieth century, as celebrated in the museum's collection. The Group of Seven was well represented. There were a few Emily Carrs.

In the middle of the century had come a brilliant explosion of talent in French Canada, and Gerry lingered in front of paintings by Jean-Paul Riopelle and Paul-Émile Borduas. The chunkiness of the latter's technique appealed more to her than the splatter of the former's, but she liked them both for their colour and energy.

"Pure art," she breathed, once again a worshipper at that altar. On the way home, staring out the train window, her brain still dazzled by all she'd seen, she resolved to set aside a little time in her own life for non-commercial work.

She drove from the train station to home, looking at objects differently, not as houses and gardens, trees and flowers, but as shapes and colours. She was still in this happy state when she pulled into her driveway and parked next to her uncle's Mercedes.

She sighed. He was sitting in his car, gripping the wheel, staring at the lake. He turned his head to meet her gaze. He looked miserable. She got out of her car quickly. "Uncle Geoff, what's happened?"

He tried to cheer up and mostly succeeded. "Gerry!" he said with a sort of fake heartiness. "Just wanted to have a word with you."

"Oh, I'm relieved. I thought someone was ill or worse, you looked so sad. Come on. You'll have to bear with me. I'm late and there are nineteen hungry cats to attend to. Can I fix you a cup of tea?"

They went inside and barricaded themselves in the kitchen while the cats agitated beyond its door. Gerry prepared cat food, made tea, grabbed some cheese straws to eat with it, and opened the door.

Geoff and she edged through the furry mass and into the next room, where they sat at the table. "Uncle Geoff, I've had the most wonderful day, looking at art, getting all inspired, realizing there's more to life than just making money."

He drank his tea and let her talk. She'd just said, "It's funny. I was just sitting here with Margaret yesterday," when he put down his cup. One by one, satiated cats drifted into the room, some just giving them a look as they passed through, others stopping to groom and settle. Mother paused by Uncle Geoff's legs, readied herself and jumped. He petted her absently.

"You don't have any pets, do you, Uncle Geoff?"

"Mary doesn't like animals." Mother began to purr, kneaded his pant leg.

Gerry spoke gently. "What is it, Uncle Geoff?"

He raised distraught eyes to look in her face. "Is it true? Do you and Prudence think your Aunt Maggie was murdered?"

"We have little evidence, Uncle Geoff, at least what the police would call evidence, but yes, we do."

"Mary says you said it had to be one of the family."

"Yes."

"But that's grotesque! That means one of us is a monster!"

"I'm sorry, Uncle Geoff, but too many little things have occurred that, taken together, can't be ignored." She told him about the teacups, the plant, and how the one cat was involved. She finished by saying, "And that's why I can't go to the police. Imagine me saying, 'One of my cats thinks its late mistress was murdered. We have the weapon. We just don't have the motive.' I'd really be the crazy cat lady at that point."

He cleared his throat and coughed. "I loved her, you know. Maggie. Oh, not romantically. It's always been Mary for me. But I know Maggie was the better person. I wish I could have loved her instead of Mary. How different things might have been. Oh well." He slowly scooped up Mother and put her on Gerry's lap. "I'll be going now. You be careful, dear. If what you suspect is true, and that person knows you suspect it, they may try to hurt you." He seemed about to say something more. "I'm sorry."

Gerry cuddled Mother in her arms as she accompanied her uncle to his car. Impulsively, she kissed his cheek through the open car window and was astonished to see tears come into his eyes.

After he left, Mother jumped down. Gone to look for Ronald, thought Gerry. Yes, where is Ronald? Not glued to Mother's side as usual. And then she and Mother saw him, rolling on the lawn with Bob and the boys. Mother paused halfway there, assessed the situation, sat, groomed, then walked away. Ronald, it seemed, had grown up.

Wednesday, Gerry made an early start: did the cats, had her coffee, and was grating carrots by the time Prudence arrived with the usual bag of baking supplies. As she took out cream cheese, a tin of pineapple and a sack each of shredded coconut, currants and walnuts, she seemed her usual self. "I hope you checked that grater for bits of aconite."

"You washed it," Gerry gently argued back. "But yes, I did. How are you?"

"Well. You?"

"Fine. Fine. I went into town yesterday, to clear my head. Looked at some art." Gerry peered down at the recipe Prudence had laid on the counter. "Four cups of grated carrot? Really?"

"It cooks down." Gerry kept grating. The extended pause told her that if Prudence was ever going to confide in her about her mother, her husband, it evidently wasn't going to be today.

Gerry sifted the dry and whisked the wet ingredients, folded in the extras at the end: pineapple, nuts, coconut, currants and, of course, the mountain of carrot. "This is going to be a big cake."

"That's why we need this." Prudence bent down and unearthed an enormous Bundt pan from one of the cupboards. She buttered and floured it before Gerry poured the batter. "Stop. That's enough. We've enough batter for a loaf as well." She prepared that pan and the cakes went into the oven. "It's a dense batter, so low and slow for a long time."

"Carrot cake with cream cheese icing. Yum."

"You can make the icing now but I'll frost the cake at the last minute. It has to be cool — "

"Or the icing will melt," Gerry finished Prudence's sentence.

"You won't need my help pretty soon," she remarked mildly.

"Oh, but what about pie, Prudence? And scones? And then Christmas is coming, so mince tarts, fruitcake — "

It was Prudence's turn to interrupt. "Okay, I get it. You want to add master baker to your list of accomplishments. Meanwhile, you should put on your art teacher hat and go get ready."

Gerry brought the six lawn chairs outside and set them in a row on the flagstone path, facing the back lawn, the wild flower garden by the shore and the lake.

The lawn gleamed wetly under a late September dew, and the garden charmed with purple asters, goldenrod, some late Queen Anne's lace, and orange bittersweet. The lake reflected the chicory blue sky and the tall pines on the far shore lent solidity to the scene.

Lucky students, she thought. And lucky me. That accomplished, she entered the gallery, started taking paintings and posters off the wall. She was pleased to have sold a few of the *Mug the Bug* prints and one of her flower miniatures, and she set those aside, along with the paintings owned by Cathy, Mr. Parminter and the Shiptons, for delivery.

Maybe I'll do that tomorrow, she thought. Or on the weekend. She looked around for Marigold and found Lightning. Gerry crouched, then sat against a wall in the dining room, let her hands lie open either side of her. The other cats in the room watched with yellow, sleepy eyes. "Come on, Lightning, I won't hurt you. Come on. How on earth did Aunt Maggie ever get you into a cat carrier to go to the vet? Maybe you trusted her."

Lightning sat, making a weird noise that alternated between high-pitched yowling and a low growl. If she'd had a tail, it would have been thrashing. As it was, her stump twitched as she prepared to spring. Gerry tensed. She let the cat wind herself up and stayed perfectly still. Then, Lightning just stopped. She sat up, licked a paw, and walked away. Progress?

It proved to be the best class yet. Entranced by the location, the students, while they may not have produced great art, thoroughly enjoyed themselves. Prudence brought the cake and tea out mid-afternoon and it was with great difficulty that Gerry shooed the students back to work. She overheard Doris remark to Gladys, "I just want to lie in a lawn chair and bask in the sun."

Gerry instructed them to purchase coloured pencils for the next class and they left, demanding she produce copies of the carrot cake recipe next time. She put away the chairs and fed the cats. As usual, Prudence had left for home during the last part of the class. Gerry peeked out the kitchen window, saw the baby carriage was gone, and sighed with relief. The world was back to normal.

She called Cathy and arranged to go over there for supper, prepared a cheque and sliced some carrot cake; was arranging it on a pretty white plate covered in pink roses when a gentle tapping on the kitchen porch door brought her to attention. She peered out and saw Andrew. Well, at least he didn't use his key and just walk in! "Andrew."

"Gerry." As she paused in the doorway, he looked uncertain. "May I come in?"

"Do you have keys to this house, Andrew?"

"Yes. I —"

"Would you mind going home and getting them, please. I'm not having anyone else —"

He held out a key ring with three keys on it. "Maggie liked to know a neighbour would be able to get in and get the cats out if there was a fire and she wasn't here. Also, I used to feed them when she or Prudence couldn't."

Gerry felt ashamed but took the keys anyway. "Would you like some carrot cake?" she mumbled. "I made it."

He smiled. "Maybe another time. Or could I take a piece home for my dessert tonight?"

She wrapped it in waxed paper. "Did you want to talk to me? Everyone else seems to."

He nodded and they went through to the next room, sat in the rockers by the fireplace. Marigold dragged herself into the room and sat between them, looking at the empty grate.

"Gerry, I'm very concerned that you may be putting yourself in danger. What if Aunt Maggie really was murdered, as you suspect? By going around talking about it, you're alerting the murderer."

"I only told your mother and sister. They told you and your father, I suppose? I can rely on Prudence to be discreet."

"My mother's been telling her friends that you've got this crazy idea and that you think one of our family did it. You know what small towns are like. I had a customer come up to me in the store today and ask if it was true." His face took on a distressed look, his brow furrowed.

Gerry spoke shortly. "Well, what's done is done, Andrew. In fact, the more people who know, the better. Maybe someone will come forward with more information."

He was silenced temporarily, then seemed to make up his mind. "About that. About coming forward. I should tell you how the Scottish lady came to be buried in your yard."

"You?"

He nodded and sank down, put his head in his hands, holding his forehead. Marigold turned. She appeared to be looking at a point beyond the top of his chair. "The morning Prudence found Maggie, she phoned me first and of course I rushed over. When I got to the bedroom I could see she was dead but I touched her anyway to make sure. I must say I didn't notice any teacup on her bedside table, spilled or otherwise, but I did notice the Doulton figurine because it was on the floor next to her bed. That didn't make sense. Did she keep it on the bedside table or the mantel? I picked it up, thinking to put it with the others downstairs, and put it in my suit pocket.

"After they took Maggie's body away, I went home and was surprised to find the figurine. I don't know why, but I felt ashamed, as though I'd stolen it. I put it in among my collection and, when I inherited Aunt Maggie's pieces, considered the matter finished. After all, it now belonged to me.

"But it bothered me. What if Prudence, who must have dusted Aunt Maggie's bedroom, remembered the thing was missing the day she died, then saw it at my place? Or you saw it there and told her? Oh, I was confused. I knew your side yard was due to be torn up so I went over one night, lifted a bit of sod and put the figurine there. I couldn't bear to break it but I thought the Hudsons would. They break everything else." Gerry nodded, thinking of her fence. "And you might even think it was old and nothing to do with Maggie. Do you understand?"

"Almost," Gerry said slowly, wondering at his delicacy of feeling about a china figurine, one among many. "That's why the third clue doesn't fit."

"What?"

"The china lady was the third sign, after the teacups, but before the plant, well, the plant sign was repeated."

"I don't know what you're talking about, about signs." He sounded bewildered.

"Don't worry, Andrew," Gerry said triumphantly, pushing the bit of cake into his hand and him and it out the door. "You've just exposed a red herring!"

Cathy had made pancakes for supper, the big thin kind, and fried mushrooms, then filled the pancakes with the mushrooms, chopped ham and grated Swiss cheese. There was even onion gravy to pour over. Gerry quickly handed over the cheque for the catering and some cash for the supper, and got down to business. "This —" she said between mouthfuls, "is — so — good." Charles thumped his tail in agreement. He'd already had his custom pancakes — ham and cheese only — mushrooms and onions not being on his list of favourite foods — but was hopeful Gerry might get careless with her cutlery and flick him some extra.

Cathy lifted her wineglass. "To a successful event!"

"To a successful event!" Gerry echoed, and drank. Then, putting down her glass, she queried, "Cathy, did you ever recall what Aunt Maggie had been afraid of or worried about? Remember, we were talking about it, before your operation?"

Cathy continued eating. "You know, one little thing came to me. It was just two words. "The boys." She mentioned "the boys" two or three times. I thought she was referring to those three cats — what are their names? — named after Second World War leaders. Winston, Franklin, and, who's the other one?"

"Joseph," Gerry replied slowly, "after the Russian, Joseph Stalin. They met at Yalta towards the end of the war."

Cathy laughed. "Yalta! That was the joke! That the three world leaders — the cats — held their meetings at Yalta down by the pool. I love it. You don't think it means anything, do you?"

"No." Gerry voice sounded distracted. No, she thought, because I don't think those are the boys Aunt Maggie was referring to. She made a note to herself to think about "the boys" later. Meanwhile, Cathy was stuffing more of the pancakes with sliced strawberries and whipped cream and Gerry settled in to enjoy the rest of her evening.

PART 4

ART

First Cat looked at the one they called Lightning and blinked slowly. After a few seconds, Lightning blinked slowly back. Then both cats turned their attention to the fireplace in the living room.

This was the room in which Maggie Coneybear had spent most autumn and winter evenings, by a small fire, surrounded by some if not all of her cats, who were drawn to the warmth and fascinated by the flickering flames, all of them postponing the moment when the fire would fade and Maggie would ascend to her cold and distant bedroom, there to switch on the electric heater and hunker down under numerous quilts overlaid with cats.

Here they were close to the kitchen, handy for late-night forays into the tub of cat kibble, or, for Maggie, to brew a last cup of tea, nibble a few cookies.

Her feet appeared first, the soles facing the cats, toes pointing upward, as though she lay in bed. Then the legs slithered down and out of the fireplace chimney, until, with a bounce, the rest of her followed. She gave herself a little shake and stood between the cats.

First Cat stood, stretched stiffly, then wound herself around where ankles should have been. Finding no contact, she gave a frustrated little "mew."

Lightning bristled and hunched her back but the woman appeared to merely laugh and shake an admonishing finger. Lightning calmed down and sat, waiting.

The woman toured the room, seemed to admire the autumn bouquet on the table, the garlands of red, yellow and blue corn *hanging in the windows. There was a pale blue bowl full of polished red apples on the mantel and she made as if to pick one up, only to see her hand pass right through it. She shrugged and moved through the passageway that led to the formal dining room. The crystal and china in the cabinets that lined the walls of the passageway tinkled as a late truck lumbered past the house.*

In the dining room she greeted the cats; wafted from one towel-lined chair to another, spending extra time looking at Mother, who dozed, alone. She winked at Bob, who winked back, and shook her head affectionately over the sleeping pile that was made up of Winston, Franklin, Joseph, and now, little Ronald.

She prowled around the room examining everything; disappeared for a moment through the wall of the gallery, only to re-emerge, smiling.

She floated from the big dining room into the foyer, checking high and low, looking for something.

First Cat and Lightning followed, mystified, as she entered the new woman's studio. Her hands passed over the various art supplies scattered on the work surface, passed over with seeming pleasure.

Then she glided with certainty to one spot in the room and pointed. First Cat walked over near the object and jumped onto the sofa. The woman became more insistent, indicating with her hands what she wanted done.

First Cat tried, reached, and fell back, exhausted, onto the sofa. Lightning jumped up beside her, leapt onto the back of the sofa and easily accomplished what First Cat could not. First Cat lurched out of the way as the object fell.

The woman clapped her hands together with pleasure, made soothing gestures at First Cat and congratulatory ones at Lightning, before she passed through the outside wall of the studio. By the time both cats had run outside, she was dissipating among the remaining leaves on the apple tree, and then she was mist between them and the stars.

15

Gerry spent Thanksgiving with Cathy and Prudence at Mr. Parminter's house. The women made the feast while Mr. Parminter provided a selection of wines. Prince Charles and Graymalkin observed an uneasy truce inside the house, while Bob and the boys and others of Gerry's bunch could be seen lurking outside, smelling turkey, and casting evil looks at Graymalkin, who, after enjoying his Thanksgiving dinner, performed an extensive grooming ritual by the sliding glass doors, then lay down in Mr. Parminter's warm kitchen for a nap, taunting the cats outside.

"I don't want to feed them here," said Gerry, "in case they start coming over even more than they already do."

"We must divide the leftovers," Mr. Parminter replied, "and you shall have extra turkey for all the furry ones. Isn't that right, Charles?" Charles, who'd eaten extremely well, even for him, burped as Mr. Parminter reached down to stroke his head. They laughed.

These are the only people I trust, thought Gerry. That's sad. That's why I need to sort this mess out with the family.

There had been no Thanksgiving invitation from Mary or Geoff. Since their talk at her house, Gerry felt that Andrew was keeping his distance, limiting contact to a wave or a smile from across the road. Of Margaret and the boys, there had been no news. Even Doug seemed to be holding back, gardening or cutting the grass when Gerry was absent.

She wondered if he was over there right now, quietly edging the perennial beds. The first few night frosts had taken the annual flowers and tender vegetables. The perennials were brown and seedy. She'd noticed they hadn't been cut back, the way she'd seen being done in other local gardens. People called it "putting the garden to bed"—a nice image. In her mind she drew a long coverlet, stretching from the lake to the house, slowly unrolling until it reached some comfy pillows nestled at the foundations—all the plants tucked in for their long winter sleep.

"That would be snow," she said aloud, chiding herself for her foolishness. Prudence and Cathy exchanged a look of amused fondness at Gerry's absent-mindedness. Mr. Parminter appeared to have heard only part of her speech.

"Sometimes right after Halloween," he said. "But never before. I remember flurries and deep cold when the children went out trick or treating, having to wear long johns under their costumes, but never snow on the ground."

"Is your house warm enough in the winter?" Gerry asked.

"Oh yes. I had it re-insulated a few years ago and that made all the difference. And I bought a new furnace. We're very comfortable here, aren't we, Graymalkin?"

The cat had returned to the living room where they were relaxing, and jumped on Mr. Parminter's lap. Cathy launched into a recital of the cute things Charles had recently done and Mr. Parminter responded with Graymalkin's antics. Gerry and Prudence quietly went to the kitchen to divide and put away the leftovers—and to tidy for Mr. Parminter.

"I wish I could afford to insulate The Maples." She picked up a tea towel. "I'm worried, Prudence, about Aunt's reference to the boys. If she was looking at those letters and then mentioned "the boys," don't you think it could have been because she thought they'd sent them?"

Prudence scrubbed at the turkey pan. "James and Geoff, possibly. David, no."

"But don't you remember, when you were young, how you wanted to be included by the older kids? I saw David look miserable when he wasn't included by his brothers. Maybe he'd do something wrong in order to fit in."

"You may be right, but if you're thinking of another confrontation, don't go on your own."

"Art class is Wednesday. Why don't we drop in on the Shaplands on Friday?"

Prudence nodded. "The morning would suit me. I'm going to visit Mother in the afternoon."

Gerry tried to keep her voice casual. "Er, how is your mother?"

"She's all right. She tells me about old friends of hers that she sees, relatives too. Apparently, your Gramma Ellie is still around. Unfinished business, Mother says."

"Any word about Aunt Maggie?" Gerry could hardly believe this conversation was happening.

"That's just it. Aunt Maggie is busy elsewhere and Gramma Ellie can't relax until they're together."

"Oh. That makes sense. Kind of."

"Apart from Mother, Mrs. Smith said she sees a dark shadow spreading through the family. A shadow cast by greed."

"Sounds like what she told me. I don't like the sound of it."

"No. Lock your doors, Gerry."

After eating turkey, mashed potatoes and pumpkin pie for a few days, it was exciting for Gerry when Prudence arrived to bake on Wednesday morning. All she had brought by way of supplies were shortening and cinnamon. "Apple pie," she said, handing Gerry an apron. "We'll make two so you can have one after the art class demolishes the first one."

One young woman, three middle-aged people and one elderly lady, plus Gerry, could certainly be depended upon to consume one pie with their afternoon tea. The people of Lovering obviously didn't care about their figures, if she was to judge by the voracious appetites of the members of her art class.

Prudence fetched the blue bowl of apples from the living room and dumped them in the sink. "I washed them," protested Gerry.

"They'll be dusty. Now, peel about sixteen and slice thinly." With the two of them working it didn't take long. They set the apples aside and began the pastry. "Recipe on the box. Ridiculously easy. I don't know what the fuss is, about making pastry. Oh, double the ingredients while you're at it.

"Now comes the delicate part. You want to work it just so you can roll it out. No kneading, just gathering and patting, then divide into two balls."

Gerry must have had the right touch because the dough coalesced into smooth lumps. "Now. Divide those two lumps into two slightly unequal lumps. You need a little more for the bottom crust than the top because of the sides." She handed Gerry the rolling pin and showed her how to strew flour across the pin and work surface. "Roll it like it has feelings, firmly but respectfully. And keep changing the angle so you get a round. We'll do both the bottoms. Good. The filling is easy. Alternate apples with a little cinnamon and sugar. Okay, set those aside. Now the top crusts. I'll show you how to crimp the edges. Fold top over bottom and pinch. Repeat."

Gerry was thrilled to find out how easy it was to produce pie crust edges that looked just like the ones she'd been eating for twenty-five years. "Now cut two slits in the middle in the shape of an X and fold back." They admired the two unbaked pies. "That's it. That's how my mother taught me. Works for pears too. Juicier fruit like plums or berries, add some corn starch to the filling, or flour if you don't have corn starch, so it thickens up."

The pies went into the oven. Soon, one of the most wonderful smells on the planet began oozing out of the kitchen into the rest of the house. They took their coffee out onto the back porch, having put on their jackets first.

"I read somewhere," Gerry began, "that if you bake a pie or bread in a house you want to sell, it can seduce prospective buyers into making an offer."

"Huh. I believe it."

"Prudence. Do you think this house needs insulation?"

Prudence nodded.

"Is it very expensive?"

She nodded again. "Not the insulation itself. It's the labour. The walls have to come down, or have many, many holes drilled into them. You should ask Doug."

"Doug seems to be avoiding me, like all the rest of my family," Gerry admitted ruefully.

"He's probably just embarrassed about his ex-wife, if he knows how she feels about you, or his sons, if it was them keyed your car."

"I hope that's all it is. I wonder if I could just do one room at a time. Maybe I could afford it then, use some of Aunt Maggie's money for that."

"I think you should save that money for emergencies. Houses always have something necessary going wrong with them and you don't want to be caught short." They finished their coffee. "Come on," Prudence said, "I'll show you what to do with the leftover raw pastry."

She gathered the scraps and rolled out a final circle, smeared it with butter and sprinkled it with brown sugar, then rolled up the dough and sliced it into inch-wide rounds. These she laid, cut side up, into another pie plate and popped in the oven. "Doo-dads," she said with a smile. "Treats for the cooks." Gerry ate two of them after her lunch and decided that they were better than apple pie.

It was a cool but sunny day so she had the art class out on the lawn again. This time they faced the house. "Draw what you see, of course," she urged, "but more importantly, draw what you feel about what you're looking at, or even what you're feeling in your life today. You can draw the whole scene or zoom in on one little thing."

Gerry drew the roofline of the house, with the chimneys poking up and the front yard's treetops draping the tiles. Then she got silly and drew all the cats, lined up on the roof's ridge, striking characteristic poses. Mother groomed Ronald, who was trying to escape; Bob and the boys were almost falling off; and Marigold was dozing, while Lightning seemed to be attacking a chimney. Others were grooming, looking at the sky, batting at flies and birds.

As they stood around eating pie, the students admired her drawing. Christine even said she might buy it, if it was for sale. Gerry critiqued their pieces gently but paused overlong looking at Judy's.

The girl had focused on the apple tree in the side yard to their left. Its leaves were gone and she'd done a good job of delineating the twigs and boughs, even the odd wizened apple that still clung in place. Yet, as Gerry looked closer, she began to see the shape of a woman, arms and legs stretched out, as though she was floating in space or water, interspersed among the twigs. "Hey, Judy, this is very clever."

Judy blushed. "You mean the tree?"

"Yes, the tree is lovely. But I mean the way you've got the form of a woman sort of mingled with the tree's parts. It's like a puzzle. One picture hidden within another."

Judy peered at her work. "Oh. That's just an accident. I didn't mean to do that. Is it good?"

Gerry was beginning to feel uncomfortable. Just there, to the right of the tree, was where the Scottish figurine had been buried, and, a little further away, was the place where Marigold had dug up the aconite. There was something a bit strange about that spot.

"Is it okay, Gerry?" Judy repeated.

"It's very good. All the more so for having been unconscious. I like it."

Judy's face flushed happily.

"Teacher's pet," Ben teased.

After they'd gone, Gerry went and stood under the apple tree, stretched out her arms and looked up into its branches. Then she fed the cats.

Gerry still felt uneasy on Thursday. She put it down to dreading visiting her cousin. When she entered the studio to work, she found that a painting, one of a group massed on the wall over the sofa, had fallen. It appeared to be undamaged, but one of the screws holding its wire to the frame had come out and she couldn't find it, though she pulled the sofa away from the wall. She leaned the painting against the sofa and tackled her work.

She was doing her best but finding the concept of *Mug the Bug* greeting cards increasingly difficult. "These just don't work," she said to herself, and pushed the morning's efforts aside. Then she grinned and quickly sketched the bug being threatened by a giant hand holding a can marked bug spray from one side, while on his other side appeared another hand wielding a large fly swatter. The text read "You think you have problems!!!" followed by "Get well soon!"

"You have a childish sense of humour," one Gerry scolded. Another Gerry replied, "I know. Ain't it great?"

She saw that Marigold had entered the room at some point and was asleep on the spot where the painting had fallen. Gerry picked it up and sat next to the cat, studying the piece.

Non-representational, it was mostly black shapes irregularly alternating with white. There was a little salmon pink, even less green. She was reminded of Judy's drawing, though that had been representational, where this was abstract. You could see so much in this, she reflected.

The signature was light grey on white and hard to make out. She sat and thought for a time. She made two phone calls. Then she tore off a length from a big roll of sketching paper and wrapped the painting, tied it with string and addressed it. She made herself a big cup of coffee, stared out the window at the lake, and waited for the courier to arrive.

16

"How do I look?" a nervous Gerry queried Prudence.

"What do you mean?" a mystified Prudence responded.

"Well, I'm about to accuse one of my cousins of the calculated murder of one of my aunts. I mean, what does one wear on such an occasion?"

"Blue jeans and a hoodie are fine," Prudence commented drily. "You're just trying to distract yourself. Are you ready?" She stood calmly by the porch door, holding her large black purse, while Gerry fidgeted, topping up the tub of kibble, feeding Marigold one more time.

"Wish us luck, Princess." She scratched the cat between its ears before grabbing her keys and finally leaving.

They drove north, through Lovering, past Geoff and Mary's street by the golf club, and continued to where the number of houses thinned out and their grandeur similarly decreased. They pulled into a dirt track driveway, its two ruts deep on either side of its grassy centre. "Whoa," said Gerry, slowing the car, "this driveway could tear off my muffler. No wonder Margaret doesn't have people over."

The house, when they finally got to it, after lurching and bumping for four or five minutes, wasn't bad. In fact, Gerry liked it and said so.

"Doug built the extension when the second and third boys came along." It was a split-level with flat roofs and Doug had cleverly doubled its size by adding on to one side a mirror image of the original.

"I don't see what's wrong with this," Gerry remarked, getting out of the car, "and it's nice and secluded, far from the road. I could live here."

"What suits you doesn't suit everybody," was Prudence's cogent reply.

"Does it hurt, being so wise?"

Prudence mock swatted at her and Gerry rang the bell.

They'd not phoned ahead, but taken a chance Margaret would be home in the morning. Sure enough, she opened the door wearing sweats, without any makeup, and with her hair hanging naturally. She looked much younger.

She must have previously looked out a window before coming to the door, because she didn't seem surprised to see them. "No cats?" she asked sarcastically, before standing aside so they could come in.

They brushed past the many coats hung off pegs in the hall before mounting half a dozen wooden steps to the living area, and, as they did, Gerry caught sight of David's worried-looking face coming out of what must have been his room in the basement. She waved and he gave a kind of half-wave in return.

The level where Margaret led them was open plan. It was furnished simply. She'd been drinking coffee at her dining table, midway between the kitchen and sitting area, and she returned to sit there. Gerry and Prudence sat down on a sofa facing her. Gerry cleared her throat and took some papers from her pocket.

"Margaret, is it possible that one or more of your sons may have written and drawn these letters to Aunt Maggie?" She carried the pile of letters to Margaret and spread them out on the table in front of her. Margaret didn't touch the letters and barely looked at them.

"It can't have been David. He's inherited the family's artistic tendencies." She fairly spat out the last few words, no doubt referring to Doug as well as Gerry.

Gerry felt relieved. She hadn't wanted it to be David. "But they could have been drawn by James or Geoff?" No response. "Where are they, anyway? I saw David."

"Out." Margaret got up and refilled her coffee. Prudence shifted on the sofa. "What's she doing here? Your bodyguard?"

Gerry sat back down, feeling rather foolish and wondering what to do now.

Prudence spoke for the first time. "Something like that. Do you think the boys might have sent these letters, hoping to please you?" Margaret became very still. "Because I've seen how hard you work to please your mother — dressing like her, serving her — and that kind of behaviour is learned by kids."

"What would you know about having kids, I'd like to know?"

Prudence flushed. "I'm older than you, Margaret, and I see things."

"So because I'm a good daughter, my sons might send nasty letters to their great-aunt? Don't be stupid."

Gerry's voice cut in. "But, Margaret, didn't they go to Maggie's to swim? That would have given them the opportunity to push letters through her door."

"Yeah, they liked to hang out at Yalta. So what? They didn't write those letters."

"So if they didn't, who did? You? Your mother?"

"Leave Mother out of it. She had nothing — "

They all paused, realizing Margaret had admitted to something. Gerry pushed. "Now you're defending her? You told me you heard her recommending an herbal tea to Aunt Maggie right before she died. What's it to be, Margaret? Your mother or you? Because I can't believe Uncle Geoff or Andrew would hurt Aunt Maggie."

Margaret looked confused and angry.

Gerry continued. "Your mother told you she'd be sure to inherit Aunt Maggie's house, didn't she? And then what was the deal? You got The Maples or your parents' present house? Or was it just going to be sold and Aunt Mary was going to give you some money?" Gerry felt cruel but she kept going. "This house not big enough for you, Margaret? Not in the right part of town? Were you jealous of Aunt Maggie, Margaret? Nice house by the river. Everybody loved her. Not like you, eh? Margaret who trails around after her abusive mother. Margaret who everybody pities and — "

"Stop!" Margaret was on her feet, hissing. "Of course Mother should have inherited. She's the last child of Grampa and Gramma Coneybear. And she was going to give it to me. Me and the boys. I love that house. I knew Grampa and Gramma. They loved me. They didn't even know you!" She was spitting out the words. "It broke their hearts when your father left — their only son."

Gerry turned pale.

Margaret continued. "Hah. Who are you? I knew Aunt Maggie before you were born. She loved *me*." Here Margaret pointed to her own chest. "If you hadn't come along — I could see how she changed toward me after you arrived — cute little baby, little five-year-old when I was pregnant, had to get married. Oh, she changed all right."

She paused, panting. "And why shouldn't I want more for my sons. David!" she screeched, and the boy, frightened-looking by now, stumbled up the stairs.

"What's happening, Mum?" he implored.

"Go outside and take that one with you." She pointed at Prudence, who was already on her feet.

"No way," Prudence snorted.

"Prudence," Gerry cautioned, staring at Margaret. "Just go outside with David and wait by the front door. Please?"

"Yeah, Prudence," mimicked Margaret, "do what your mistress says."

Prudence turned and took David's arm, led him, protesting, down the stairs, slammed the door. Gerry could hear David's voice from outside, but not what he was saying.

"That's why David's never come over — he didn't want to displease you," Gerry said slowly.

"Bad enough my former husband is slinking around you. Bitch." Margaret said the last word calmly and sat back down at the table.

"He's not slinking. He does the garden and the grass, same as he did for Aunt Maggie. Margaret, why did you clear the room except for the two of us?"

"Because I want you to hear how I did it."

Gerry felt sick to her stomach and sank back down onto the sofa. "Oh, Margaret," she said softly, and realized that she'd never really believed her cousin, or anyone else, could kill her aunt. She'd just been playing a silly game of detection, with Prudence for audience, had hoped Margaret would admit to the letters perhaps, and nothing more.

Margaret fiddled with her empty coffee cup, running one index finger round and round the rim. "Mummy's got loads of gardening books, just like Maggie had."

Gerry felt a cold chill as Margaret's voice slipped into a childlike one, and she resumed using the familiar "Mummy."

"I just looked in those, at the pictures, found the ones in Mummy's garden that are poisonous and picked one." Margaret continued in a dreamlike tone. "I wanted one where she'd just go to sleep. I didn't want her to suffer. It was so easy. She phoned up Mummy, saying she couldn't sleep and Mummy sent me over with an herbal tea she'd bought."

Gerry interrupted her. "So Aunt Mary knows you went over there. But she didn't say anything when I was at her house."

Margaret laughed. "She's not going to help you! I took the herbal tea, but I gave Aunt Maggie something else, yes, I did." She hugged herself. "I had had it ready for weeks, the roots. All I had to do was make the tea." She frowned and her voice became querulous. "But she wouldn't drink it. She said it smelled nasty. She said, 'Just

leave it there, Margaret, and maybe I'll drink it later.' Ordering me."
Her voice became small again. "Just like Mummy does."

Gerry waited, barely breathing. "And then what happened?"

"I went home." Margaret straightened up and sounded like
her usual sarcastic self again. "She wasn't going to drink it with
me standing there. So I left. She was still alive when I left. But she
must have drunk it later, and the best part is, you don't even know
about—" She stopped herself and looked triumphantly at Gerry.

"I don't even know about what, Margaret?"

Margaret just laughed. There was nothing left for Gerry to
say. On the step outside she found Prudence alone. "Where did
David go?"

"He took off into the woods. He's very upset. Are you all right?"

"Me? I'm fine. Except I feel a bit sick to my stomach. I hope
David goes to Doug. Come on, Prudence. Let's go home. I'll tell
you what she said on the way."

Neither of them got much work done that afternoon. They tried
to puzzle out if there was any way to prove any of what Margaret
had said. By speaking only with Gerry, she'd made it one person's
word against the other's. And to top it all off, Gerry received a
vituperative call from Mary, claiming that Margaret was so
hysterical that she and Geoff were thinking of taking her to the
hospital if they couldn't get her to calm down.

"Where are you calling from?" Gerry asked.

"Our house. Why?"

"Well, if she was together enough to drive to your place, she
can't be all that hysterical," Gerry concluded. That didn't go over
well. An enraged Aunt Mary shrieked into the phone and hung up.

"I should have spoken to Uncle Geoff," muttered Gerry. "He's
the only one there with any sense. Prudence, you might as well go
home. I'll do the cats tonight."

"Are you sure?"

"Yes. We're both tired and shocked and need to rest. Let Uncle Geoff deal with those two. I've had it."

That evening neither Gerry nor the cats could settle. She trudged from room to room; taking a book, then putting it back; lifting up some of the family china, wondering when she'd ever use it. The cats, some of them, took turns accompanying her. Of course, they still needed their sleep, but when Marigold tired, Lightning took her place (much to Gerry's surprise); when Bob went outside, Ronald showed up; and so on until well after midnight when Gerry found herself sitting in her pyjamas, robe and slippers on the grand staircase staring down into the hall.

The hall was as big as a room. She'd never taken it in from this vantage point, and at this time of night, and in her frame of mind, she found it utterly gloomy. She peered through the heavy wooden railings at the dark red wallpaper, only slightly illuminated by antique wall sconces that looked crookedly mounted. The wispy sheer curtains over the front entrance's windows shifted slightly, as though someone had brushed by them.

She reached over and picked Ronald up and put him on her lap. Absently, she also reached over and began stroking Lightning, then drew back her hand in alarm. But Lightning, while not purring like Ronald, hadn't reacted as though Gerry were trying to kill her, but continued to sit placidly. Gerry said nothing, but smiled a little and resumed stroking. Progress!

She wasn't sleepy but went up to bed, lay there for hours before she slept for a bit.

Saturday, she tried to settle to work, but was unsuccessful, got so nervous she drove to a nearby flea market and wandered from stall to stall, looking at overpriced antiques and junk, bought a bag of candy from one merchant and some donuts from another, before devouring a good, home-style burger — with everything.

When she got home, she slept for most of the afternoon and awoke feeling better, was able to work on the painting of

Bea's pansy orchid. She thought it would make a nice Christmas present for her.

As always, when she was absorbed in work, time passed unnoticed — but not by the cats, who gave her half an hour past their usual supper hour, then began scratching at the studio door.

As she passed through the entranceway on her way to the kitchen, the last rays of the setting sun slanted in through the windows and the filmy curtains, illuminating the spot where she'd sat so sadly the night before. "The sun! The sun!" she sang as she fed the cats, and her mood lightened.

Sunday was better, a cool, crisp autumn day. The furnace had kicked in during the night, so she turned the thermostat down and made a fire in the living room. This proved to be a magnet for the cats, who chose radiant heat over forced air and joined her.

She read a book about perennials and their management, and realized her beds could be left uncut for several reasons. After reading the passage, she hoped Doug was leaving them like that on purpose and wasn't just busy elsewhere. She'd have to ask him next time she saw him.

For one thing, snow accumulated more efficiently to cover the roots if some of the top structure of the plant was left. Secondly, and this was the reason Gerry liked the best, the dried seed heads offered some sustenance to over-wintering birds. Thirdly, the garden looked nice. There were some photographs of the winter garden, its bare bones draped with snow.

She reached for her sketch pad and doodled. The phone rang. "Ah, hello?" she said distractedly, dragged back to reality. Andrew was speaking. She looked out the roadside window.

"Gerry, my father is missing." His voice, usually so steady, cracked. Gerry didn't have a response for that. "Gerry? Gerry? Are you there?"

"What?" was all she managed.

He spoke carefully. "My mother just phoned me. He was at home yesterday." His tone became bitter. "That's the last time she remembers seeing him. Careless of her, to lose her husband."

"Andrew, is Margaret with your mother?"

"Uh, no. She's at her house, as far as I know."

"Do you know if there was a scene, or scenes, rather, on Friday?"

"I heard something about it," he replied cautiously.

"I believe Margaret's unbalanced, Andrew. You should check her first, see if Uncle Geoff's there. Call me when you've been there, if you like."

"Right."

Gerry put down the phone with a sinking feeling in her stomach. Just when she'd gotten over Friday's revelations. "Drat!" she told the cats. "What next?"

Next was another call from Andrew. "Margaret's in bed. She's not saying much. What?" He appeared to be speaking with someone. Gerry waited. "Gerry?"

Gerry could hear, by the change in his voice, that something more was coming. "I'm here, Andrew. What is it?"

"Mother came with me. She's just informed me that Dad went out hunting yesterday." He spoke to Mary. "How could you not think of that until now?"

Gerry heard her irritated response. "I just thought he'd gone out to have some fun. Left me to hold everything together here."

Andrew's voice dripped with exasperation. "When has he ever done that, Mother?" He switched back to Gerry. "I think my father's in the woods. He may have injured himself."

"Andrew, I met him up near the sugar shack a few weeks ago. He'd shot some birds. He said he couldn't walk as far as he used to and had parked over in that development near the tracks and walked in."

"Right. I'll go and see if his car's there."

Gerry grabbed her jacket from where it hung in the kitchen porch. "I'll come on foot from this end and meet you by the shack." They both hung up.

Gerry stuffed a bottle of water and a flashlight into her pockets and, with a shouted "Sorry, cats, I may be late!" stumbled outside.

Across the road, Andrew's house had that stillness common to unoccupied places. She looked at Mr. Parminter's frontage, hoping for a glimpse of Graymalkin. Only Mr. Parminter's curtains, drawn for the night, showed her someone was home.

As she half ran, half walked up the lane toward the woods, Cathy's house presented a livelier appearance. Lights shone in the front rooms as well as upstairs, and several parked cars indicated the B&B was having a busy weekend. Gerry thought she heard Prince Charles's basset tones and smiled. She wished she was headed for a convivial supper with Cathy and the prince.

The sun was low, directly in front of her as she continued to where the lane ended and the trail began. Old fence posts aslant in the ground and bits of rusty barbed wire reminded her these were relatively new woods; that all this land had once been for crops or pasture, possibly land her family had farmed once upon a time.

She smelled the steeped tea odour of damp fallen leaves and dying ferns. She'd forgotten her rubber boots and her sneakers and socks were soon soaked as she moved through wet underbrush and muddy puddles.

She came to the train tracks, turned and jogged the length of one field and then another. Faster than going through the woods and more light. The sun was almost gone. The railway ties were set just the wrong distance apart for her tempo and it hurt as her feet repeatedly slipped off them onto the large rocks between. The creosote-soaked ties gleamed black against the pink and grey of the rocks.

The trail to the sugar shack sloped down to her left. Far away, down the tracks just before they curved out of sight, she could see a tall figure coming toward her. Andrew, still a few minutes away. Minutes might count if Uncle Geoff had had an accident, a heart attack. She would go in ahead of Andrew. She clicked on her flashlight.

Her feet thanked her as she moved off the tracks and onto soft soil. Here was the old growth forest, giant trees you couldn't get two people's linked arms to meet around. More conifers too: hemlock, cedar. She flashed her light around and cursed. It lit up only ten feet in front of her, would save her tripping on a stone or root, but would be useless for looking for her uncle. Why hadn't she thought to grab the heavy-duty emergency light from her car's trunk?

She rattled the lock on the sugar shack door. Shut. She ran around to a side window. Boarded up. The back? Ah. Here the boards had been partially pried away, probably by kids. She shone her light into the shack. "Uncle Geoff?" Where was Andrew?

She lifted her leg, balanced on one knee on the window frame, stuck her head inside. Something rustled in a far corner. "Uncle Geoff?" She heard her voice, tremulous, and shone her light. The rustle was coming closer. An animal?

"Holy shit!" she yelled and threw herself backward, landing awkwardly, half-sprawled against a stump, before falling sideways onto the ground. The wall of the shack almost completely saved her.

The skunk sprayed the interior of the shack, having aimed toward the window. Gerry got up and ran back to the path in front. She'd dropped her flashlight when she'd fallen. She stood there in the dark as the terrible smell permeated the forest. "He's not in there," she was able to tell a breathless Andrew.

"I heard you yell," he panted, bent over from his effort. "I'm not as fit as I thought I was, obviously." He waved his hand in front of his nose. "God, you smell terrible."

"It's not all me," a furious Gerry replied. "It sprayed the whole shack!"

Andrew's light was powerful, and he was able to shine it well into the woods either side of the path as they made their way up the hill through the sugar bush. Andrew asked, "Where could he be? His car was where you said it might be. What if he's not out here? Where could he have gone? What's happening, Gerry?"

"I'm not sure, Andrew. I only know part of it, I guess. Just keep looking."

They reached the top of the hill and walked through a plantation of pine. It was colder in there and fallen needles muffled their footsteps. Gerry didn't like the darkness or the rigidity of the neat rows. "He planted this, you know," Andrew said softly. "He liked to — " But Gerry had grabbed his arm, was pointing.

17

It took a lot of gentle pleading with Andrew to get him to leave what was left of his father. The shotgun blast had taken most of the head, but Andrew wanted to touch him anyway. "Best not to, Andrew," Gerry said through her tears. "He's not here. He's not here."

"I'll stay while you get the police," he stubbornly insisted, his face turned away as he leaned on a tree, and Gerry was reminded of the honour guard of cats surrounding her aunt's dead body, who still slept on her bed.

"Your family needs you," she stated. "You don't want me to tell them, do you?" This seemed to penetrate and he allowed her to lead him away.

There was no longer any need for haste. At the tracks they turned left, towards where Andrew and Uncle Geoff's cars waited. They walked in silence, and Gerry, arm in arm with Andrew, stuck her free hand in her coat pocket. She found the pack of candy she'd bought — what? — just the day before? "Here. We're both in shock. Eat some of these." She handed him some sour gummy worms.

He started shaking with laughter. "Who eats these when they're grown up? You bought these?"

"Andrew, Andrew, calm down. Here, drink this." She handed him the water bottle and saw the tears running down his face. He drank and she awkwardly patted him on the shoulder.

They left Uncle Geoff's car where it was parked; the police might want to examine it. Gerry drove Andrew's. He was shaking his head and muttering, "I don't believe it. I don't believe it. He must have slipped and the gun went off. Christ, poor Mother." He had his face in his hands when they bumped along Margaret's driveway.

Gerry stayed in the car. "Andrew, I know you're family and I should be able to come in, but I don't feel I'd be welcome. In fact, I'm sure I wouldn't be. So I'll just take your car and park it at your house. You can call me if you need a ride. Okay?"

He nodded dumbly and entered the house.

Why can't I have a nice, normal family like everybody else? Gerry wondered.

When she got home she dropped her stinky coat outside, made a cup of tea and phoned Prudence. After her initial astonishment, Prudence quietly said, "We better get baking."

"Baking!" Gerry faintly replied.

"There'll be a visitation before and a reception after the funeral. People need something sweet at times like these. You go ahead and have a long hot bath and we'll make something really good tomorrow."

"I don't think I can face the students this week."

"Wait until tomorrow, then phone and cancel. By then they'll have mostly heard and you won't have to break the news five separate times."

"Were you related to Uncle Geoff, Prudence?" Gerry's throat constricted when she said his name and she blew her nose.

"I don't think so, not by blood, but he was my cousin's husband and a good man. Not many like him."

They said their goodnights and Gerry did as she had been told: ran a deep bath with plenty of bubbles. She left the bathroom door a little open and wasn't surprised when a few cats came in to investigate. Winnie, Frank and Joe, with their new sidekick Ronald, were fascinated by the shifting foam and sat on the bathtub edge, batting with tentative paws.

Gerry had placed a box of tissues near the bath, but didn't need as many as she'd thought she would; watching the cats' absorption distracted her and she even smiled, albeit weakly.

Perhaps because of the bath, the shock, or the run up into the woods, sleep came easily. The phone's insistent ringing woke her. It was the police.

She told the officer of her meeting Andrew by the sugar shack and of them finding Uncle Geoff's body together. The only questions he asked were whether they'd touched the gun or the body — no, and no — and if she'd noticed her uncle had been upset or depressed lately — no, again. Then he wished her good day. Then she remembered how unhappy Uncle Geoff had been when he'd been sitting in his car at her place and wondered if she'd been completely honest with the officer.

She phoned Andrew. "How are you today?"

He sounded exhausted. "Worse. Did you talk with the police?"

"Yes."

"They're thinking it's an accident or suicide."

Gerry paused. "How's your mother?"

"Coping."

"Let me know if I can help, Andrew."

"I will. Goodbye."

Gerry shuffled around, making coffee, feeding cats, and was still in her robe when Prudence arrived. Prudence looked her usual self, in her grey pants and white blouse. She did the cat boxes and tidied the kitchen while Gerry slowly dressed and came downstairs.

"What are we making today?" she wearily asked.

"I don't have a name for them. They're just 'those wonderful squares you make.' I always take them to funerals. They'll give you a toothache, they're so sweet."

"Sounds good. What do I do?"

"You start with a shortbread crust. We'll double the recipe and use this big pan."

As Gerry assembled the shortbread — brown sugar, butter, flour — and pressed it into the pan, Prudence remarked casually, "I was thinking I might use some of your aunt's legacy to me to buy a little car."

"Oh, Prudence, what a good idea. Then you won't have to walk that carriage along the road anymore. I was wondering how you managed in winter. Now what?"

"We bake it. It's the base for this." She took two cans of sweetened condensed milk from her bag. "The magic ingredient. We're going to make caramel." They each took a can and dumped the contents into a pot, scraping out the cans with spoons, although some of the Gerry's can's contents somehow managed to make it into her mouth. They added butter, corn syrup and vanilla, and cooked the concoction over low heat for about five minutes, stirring continuously and watching for bubbles. Then they poured it over the cooked cookie base and baked it again.

While they waited for it to turn golden brown, they did the dishes. "The only thing," Prudence began slowly.

"Yes?"

"The only thing about getting a car is — I can't drive!" They looked at each other and laughed.

"I'll teach you, Prudence."

"I have to take lessons from an accredited driving school."

"Well, I'll let you practise on my car between lessons."

"Would you? That'd be great. I was worried about how I'd practise. Thank you."

The dessert came out of the pan smelling like candy. "It takes a while to cool," Prudence cautioned.

"You don't mean — we're going to ice it too?"

Prudence nodded. "Chocolate."

Gerry phoned her students and reassured them that she would be able to teach them the following week. Andrew called to say the visitation would be Wednesday afternoon and evening. Cathy called as soon as she heard and invited Gerry to dinner that night. "No charge, my dear. Just some TLC from me to you." Gerry hung up with tears in her eyes. Bea phoned to make the same offer and Gerry arranged to see her on the following evening.

Gerry went over to Mr. Parminter's after lunch to break the news personally, but he'd already heard. Someone had phoned him. All he could say was, "Terrible thing. It's a terrible thing," as he patted Graymalkin, asleep on his lap. Gerry asked him if he wanted to go to the visitation but he declined, accepting a ride to the funeral instead. She made him a cup of tea and went home.

Prudence was icing the caramel. "They're wicked hard to cut. I'll do it the day of the visitation and we'll arrange them on a plate."

"Don't come to work on Wednesday, Prudence. I'll cut the squares and pick you up in the afternoon and we can go together. They're less likely to throw both of us out."

Prudence nodded. "I'll just do the cats and then I'll be off."

Gerry caught her hand. "Thank you. It really helped. The baking."

Prudence said no more, just looked pleased.

Gerry was so tired she drove the short distance to Cathy's house. Her friend must have been watching for her, because she opened the front door and welcomed Gerry in. "I thought we could have a drink and snacks in the living room first."

Candles glowed in the large, shabbily elegant room. Charles sprawled in front of a fire.

"Don't get up, Charles," Gerry exhorted. He didn't, but showed, by his tail whacking the floor a couple of times when she bent down and scrunched him between the ears, that she was welcome.

"What you need is a g and t," Cathy said, offering her one.

Gerry collapsed in a comfy chair with a sigh. "Bless you. You're a saint."

Cathy sat down across from her, Charles between them, and passed Gerry a little bowl of cashews. "We don't have to talk about it unless you want to."

"Good. I spent the morning on the phone and Prudence and I baked some squares for Wednesday. I cancelled the art class. I feel organized but lost at the same time."

"You're allowed. For supper we have roast chicken, mashed potatoes and green beans with little crispy bits of bacon and almonds. It's all done. Just tell me when you're ready."

Gerry jumped up, astonishing Charles. "Ready!"

Tuesday morning she took more calls. Some of her clients phoned their condolences. Andrew called to say he thought the funeral would be on Saturday.

She looked through her cupboard. The little black dress wasn't appropriate. And the weather was too cool to wear the navy skirt she'd worn to Aunt Maggie's funeral. She drove to a shopping centre and bought some black dress pants, black flats and an ivory sweater with little pearl buttons running down the front. As she drove home along the river road, dead leaves skittered in front of the car. The herons, wading by the shore, were long gone, flown to wherever herons went for the winter. Instead, hundreds of Canada geese floated, awaiting the signal that would send them south. Her windshield wipers flicked steadily at a few raindrops and by the time she got home, she was ready for a nap.

She was late feeding the cats and she was late arriving at Cece and Bea's for supper. "Sorry, sorry. I seem to be moving in slow motion."

"Delayed reaction," said Cece, opening a bottle of red wine. "I heard from Andrew how you held it together, got him to the car, drove to Margaret's. Well done." He toasted her.

She felt herself well up. "Not my dad," she mumbled. "I knew how he must be feeling, that's all."

Bea slid a box of tissues in her direction before remarking quietly, "Every death reminds us of all the other deaths."

"Who said that?" Gerry asked, wiping her eyes, thinking of her parents, Aunt Maggie, and now, Uncle Geoff.

"Why, I believe it was Bea Muxworthy," her friend replied, putting a serving of lasagne in front of Gerry. Gerry laughed shakily and blew her nose.

The lasagne was just what she needed, as was the bowl of expensive ice cream that followed. They turned on the TV and watched a boring documentary about the American Civil War. Gerry fell asleep in the recliner while Bea and Cece snuggled on the chaise longue.

"I'm sorry to be the one to have to tell you, but you snore," Bea teased, as Cece helped Gerry on with her coat.

"Hah! She should talk. Talk about the night train!" Cece stepped outside with Gerry while Bea waved from the doorway.

The drizzle had stopped and the stars showed themselves. Gerry took a deep breath. "You don't notice fresh air after a while."

Cece closed the car door. She lowered the window. "Anything you need to tell me, Gerry?"

She didn't understand at first, then realized he was referring to Uncle Geoff's death. "No. No. I don't think so, Cece," she said gravely. "But I really should make my will soon, don't you think? Thanks for a lovely evening." Soberly, she drove away.

She spent the next morning with *Mug the Bug*, planning his next move. Halloween was coming. How could she incorporate that in her next few strips? Like most comic artists, she worked a few weeks in advance, to allow for holidays and illnesses. And deaths.

After lunch, she cut the squares. Prudence had been right: wicked hard to cut. Fortunately, Prudence had taped a note to the plastic wrap covering them. Use the big chef's knife and wash it after each cut. Even following these instructions, bits of caramel stuck to the knife. Obviously, Gerry decided, these were meant to be scraped off with a fork and then into the cook's mouth. Stickily, she arranged the squares on a big tray and re-covered them, put them in her trunk. Then she changed and left to get Prudence.

Gone were the salmon-pink geraniums from Prudence's little house's window boxes. Instead, she'd placed scarlet-leafed Virginia creeper. A family of robins were pecking at its grapelike fruit. They dispersed when Prudence came out her front door. "Makes them drunk," she said, sliding into the front seat.

"What?"

"The fermenting berries make the birds drunk. Wild grapes are the worst. Once I saw crows falling off a fence, they were so inebriated."

Gerry paused, looking at Prudence. "You have just given me the mental image required for my next painting. 'Drunk Crows.'" She put the car in gear and they drove slowly to Lovering's small funeral parlour.

Located in an old house, it was comforting to enter, as though they really were visiting Uncle Geoff at somebody's home. They took off their coats, signed the book in the hall, and handed the tray to one of the young workers. "Parsley?" Gerry whispered. Prudence smiled a ghost of a smile and nodded.

The coffin, bedecked with wreaths and bouquets, was in the main room. There were quite a few people milling around with a cup in one hand and something sweet in the other. Gerry and Prudence stood uneasily until Andrew came over, led them to where the rest of the family were.

It was all very civilized.

Aunt Mary stood. She and Gerry carefully kissed the air either side of the other's cheeks, equally carefully refraining from touching; made little inarticulate sounds at each other.

Margaret, sitting behind her mother, looked dazed, as though she'd been drugged. Her sons stood around her, looking frightened. Gerry said, "Margaret," and, when there was no reaction, approached the boys. They permitted her to hug them. David clung.

Andrew gave her a grave kiss on the cheek and thanked her for coming. And that was it.

She and Prudence got themselves a cup of coffee and a square and mingled. Gerry wondered if Doug would come. The atmosphere was subdued. People spoke quietly as they greeted each other.

After twenty minutes, they reversed the order of their actions: put down their cups, said goodbye to the Petherbridges, paused by the coffin, and took their coats from the young attendant.

There wasn't much to say. As Gerry drove Prudence home, rain began to fall again.

When she got home, the answer to one of her questions was waiting.

18

Dear Gerry,
*   This is what I wish you to present to the police, if there is ever any question about Maggie Coneybear's death being suspicious.*

Geoff

Since her sister inherited The Maples, my wife, Mary Coneybear Petherbridge, has made my life hell. She had been led to believe by her mother, Ellie Catford Coneybear, that the house would be left to Mary and Maggie equally. Perhaps this was my mother-in-law's intention. In any case, when she died, this assumption was found to be false. Everything, except for a cash legacy, went to the younger sister.

Mary brought up our children, Margaret and Andrew, to resent their Aunt Maggie. It worked with Margaret, not with Andrew. This resentment has poisoned our family life, both at home and in the community, as people were able to see for themselves what kind of a person Maggie was and Mary is.

Nevertheless, my first allegiance has always been to my wife and children, so when I was told by Maggie that instead of leaving The Maples to Mary, she was going to change her will to leave everything to Gerry Coneybear, our niece, I felt I had to act to prevent this.

My son Andrew will attest that sales at our store have been poor and we are faced with shutting down. My wife's extravagant lifestyle has left us with a large mortgage, car loans and little cash in hand. We have also been supporting in part my daughter Margaret and her children.

Unbeknownst to me, Maggie had either already changed her will and was, perhaps, trying to prepare me, or changed it shortly thereafter. I didn't know that and went ahead with preparations to kill her.

I'd always liked my sister-in-law and wished her to suffer as little as possible. I'd heard my wife talking about poisonous plants to one of her friends and noted which ones they were. I prepared the root of the aconite plant.

The night my sister-in-law died, I heard my wife again discussing plants with her sister on the phone, this time recommending an herbal tea for insomnia. After she'd gone to bed, I drove to my sister-in-law's house with the aconite.

Though surprised to see me, she accepted that Mary had sent me with a remedy. I told her to go to bed and I would bring her the tea. I added a bag of black tea to the aconite to disguise the flavour.

I placed the cup on her bedside table. She took a couple of sips, said it tasted funny and put it down. I joked about not even being able to make a cup of tea and left.

At home, I went into my study, and turned on the TV. Eventually, I dozed off in my chair. My wife Mary found me there the next morning, when she came to tell me that her sister was dead. She was very excited and remarked, "Now we'll get what we've always deserved."

A few days later, I admired her control when we found out everything had been left to Gerry.

Gerry, I was going to kill you when I met you in the woods a few weeks ago. I'd heard from Cece Muxworthy that

you hadn't yet made a will, and knew Mary would inherit if
you died without one. I reasoned that you'd hardly be likely
to leave your estate to her when you got around to making a
will. I'm sorry. But I'm glad I didn't kill you. It was bad enough
what I did to Maggie. And for nothing.

To my wife, I can only say, "I hope you get what you
deserve." If they rule accidental death, you'll get the life
insurance. If the verdict is suicide, you get nothing.

I plan to go up to the woods now, and end it that way. To
my son Andrew, I'm sorry. To my grandsons, I love you. Be
good men.

Geoff Petherbridge

"I don't believe it," Gerry said. She stood with the letter in her
hand in the front hall. As she'd read, the envelope had dropped
from her hand. She picked it up now and walked stiffly to the
stairs and sat down. "Uncle Geoff kill Aunt Maggie? Kill me? He
couldn't. He wouldn't. He wouldn't kill for money, for a lifestyle!"
She burst into tears and rocked herself, feeling miserable.

She gathered the rest of the mail off the front door mat and
plodded into the kitchen. Whatever happened, cats still needed to
eat. "This has been," she said to their expectant faces, "one hell of
a long day." She made tea and fed them, then wandered away into
her studio.

The late afternoon sun slanted in across her worktable and
onto the rug in front of the fireplace. She switched on the electric
heater and sat on the sofa, drinking her tea.

She wondered what the verdict had been — accidental death
or suicide — but maybe it was too soon for anyone to have decided.
She flipped through the rest of her mail, handling the envelope
Uncle Geoff's letter had come in again. Wait a minute, her fingers
told her. It's too thick. She extracted another letter.

Dear Gerry,

This is what I wish you to show the police if Margaret is not brought under control, or if she ever endangers anyone again. I am not at present fearful for the boys' safety, but you never know. Use this if you have to.

Geoff

My daughter, Margaret Petherbridge Shapland, poisoned her aunt, Maggie Coneybear. She admitted this to me at her house last Friday night after her mother had gone home.

Margaret was very upset after a visit from you, Gerry, and Prudence Crick, during which you accused her of this crime. Her mother and I stayed with her all day. Her mother got tired and went home while I prepared to sleep on the sofa to watch over Margaret.

But Margaret couldn't sleep and seemed to want to talk. She claimed that her mother had assured her they would inherit The Maples this time, whenever Aunt Maggie died. When I asked her why she had done it, she said something about not wanting Mummy to have to wait any longer.

My daughter is a very disturbed person, made so by years of living with a capricious, demanding, and unloving mother. Those years have destroyed her, as they have me.

I remonstrated with her, assuring her that while we have some debts we have enough credit to get by on. But I doubt she did it for the house and money, though she loves The Maples, and could always use more money, but rather as a bid to please her mother.

She described how she looked up the poisonous plants, made her selection, and prepared the roots. Then she waited her chance. As she told you, Gerry, she went over to Maggie's with an offering of herb tea, and when she left, her aunt was dying but not dead.

I can't bear to think of poor Maggie lying there, feeling ill, beginning to realize Margaret has poisoned her. And wanting to get out of bed, get to a phone, but being paralyzed; having to watch her life run out. I can't think of it without a shudder, that it was my daughter, my little girl! who did this horrible thing.

After Margaret told me all this, I made her promise not to tell anyone, especially her mother. I said her mother would be angry and hate her if she knew her daughter had murdered her sister. And I hoped it was true.

When Mary told me her sister was dead, she was sad, but she was also excited to inherit her estate. It has been a disappointment to her. I love and pity my daughter. I am no longer sure how I feel toward my wife.

That day we met in the woods, I was trying to get up the courage to kill myself. I killed the birds so it would look like an accident and Mary would get the life insurance. I'd already written a version of the other letter and left it in my desk. I meant to protect Margaret. I hope she gets the care she needs. I have indicated her need for this in a letter to Andrew.

But you met me in the woods, Gerry, and I could hardly explain what I meant to do. I'm sorry this has been so unpleasant for you. I hope things improve for my family in the future. I know your future will be bright.

Affectionately,
Geoff Petherbridge

"Oh, poor Uncle Geoff!" Gerry moaned, leaning her forehead on one hand.

She left her tea unfinished, pushed both letters back into their envelope, and rushed to the bank, passing the funeral home once more, where the Petherbridges were still holding the visitation. With shaking hands she placed the envelope into her safety deposit box.

It was only when she got home again and examined the rest of her mail that she found the confirmation of what else she'd suspected.

Andrew had closed the store for the week, so Gerry knew he'd most likely be free when she invited him over Thursday afternoon. She made a pot of coffee and a fire in the living room and they sat in the rockers by the hearth.

"Are the funeral arrangements done?"

He nodded. "It's Saturday afternoon. Be there?"

"Of course." They rocked for a bit. Marigold sat on Gerry while Ronald, to her surprise of all the cats, had climbed onto Andrew. "It's my mother's birthday today," Gerry said in a pensive voice. "She'd be fifty-five."

"How old was she when she died?"

"Forty-four. It's been eleven years. I can't believe it." She stroked Marigold and the little cat shivered.

"Cats are very therapeutic," Andrew remarked. Ronald began a robust purr that seemed at odds with his thin frame.

"Unless they're hungry and you want to sleep in. Or if they're barfing hair balls all over the rugs." Gerry smiled. "No. I agree. Therapeutic. Andrew, I wanted to ask you, will your family be okay financially? What if the life insurance doesn't pay out?"

He replied grimly, "Mother will just have to sell her big house and take an apartment somewhere."

"But the business, the store — they're all right?"

"Actually, I'm thinking of selling the store, closing the shop, that is. We only employ old Mrs. Wilson and she's ready to retire. I'd like to start a design business, source furniture and accessories for people."

"That sounds like fun." Gerry broached the next topic carefully, keeping her voice neutral. "And Margaret?"

His face became serious. "I think Margaret will be going away. Dad left me a letter — " he choked up a bit — "in which he expressed how he thought she might be a danger to herself, the boys. And she's certainly shown signs of that the last few days before Dad died, according to Mother and the boys; either ranting about Aunt Maggie and you, or curling up into a ball. She's gone into herself since…since the accident. She won't speak, just stares at nothing. Mother and I agree we'll have to place Margaret in a residence. Nearby, so we can visit. The boys can't care for her. Doug will move in with them for a while. After all, it's his house too, or used to be."

Gerry leaned forward and took one of Andrew's hands. "Andrew, it's very important you pay attention to what your father thought about Margaret. He also told me he thought she should be put away." Then she added in a faraway voice. "It's all very sad. I got a letter, too, yesterday, Andrew, from an independent art appraiser." She grew pensive as she mused, "I think Margaret knew…" then she brightened. "You'll never guess what."

The funeral was held in the large church near Geoff and Mary's home. Gerry and Prudence sat among the numerous cousins of the Petherbridge and Coneybear families.

Afterwards, the church ladies outdid themselves. A magnificent tea was held in the adjacent hall: crustless sandwiches and an endless variety of mouth-watering squares and miniature tarts, rivalling even Prudence's wonderful caramel treats, were set out on long tables.

Gerry tried not to overindulge, but smiling ladies kept circulating with trays, urging her to take just one more.

Margaret did not attend. Gossip was that she'd completely broken down under the strain of losing her father. Gerry listened and nodded, offered nothing in the way of information to any of the gently curious. Perhaps Margaret had always been a trouble to her family, she thought.

She drove Mr. Parminter and Prudence home and collapsed, completely exhausted, only to see it was time to feed the cats. All were present except Marigold.

She checked the house. No cat. Then she went outside. Marigold was sitting under the apple tree, looking up into its bare branches. "Hello, sweetheart," Gerry said, relieved, and reached to pick her up. Marigold evaded her and walked into the garden.

The cat sat on a flagstone and surveyed her domain. Late purple asters still bloomed and she touched her nose to a few that drooped over the path. She looked beautiful in the autumn garden, her bright white, reddish brown and black providing a focal spot among the perennials dying back to beiges and greys. She circled the sundial, then walked down towards Yalta. Gerry followed.

Marigold crouched by the ivy-covered fence and looked at the now empty pool, where a few leaves blew, then settled.

She walked slowly through the gate back onto the lawn and sat again, as if she were trying to make up her mind. Then, ignoring the hydrangea bush, now just a shock of brittle sticks topped with lacy bronze flower heads, she moved towards the wasteland behind the shed and began to creep into a thicket.

"No, you don't," said Gerry, pulling her out. "I'd never get you out of there. Want your supper?"

When they got back to the kitchen, the hungry horde had finished, but Marigold did not eat. Worried, Gerry kept an eye on her for the rest of the evening, carried her up to bed. Marigold couldn't settle, jumped off the bed and left Gerry's room.

"Fine," said a weary Gerry to Bob, rolling at her feet. "We're fine as we are, right, Bob?" He stared at her with his round yellow eyes, gave another mock bite on her feet and went to sleep.

When she woke, Gerry's first thought was the cat. Not there, next to her, a warmth nestled into the curve of her belly. Not anywhere downstairs. Must be outside again, she thought, feeding the others, but, when she looked, she couldn't find her, not even in the thicket between The Maples and the abandoned house next door.

"That's funny," she said to herself, picking burrs off her pants and sweater. She went inside and made coffee, and was going to sit in the living room when she saw the door to the cupboard under the stairs was a bit ajar. "Marigold?" she called as she swung it wide. "Oh, God."

She knelt by the little thing, flat as a rag, a small damp patch on the floor under her rear end. She was breathing harshly and her jaw was fixed in a rictus, stiff, lips curled back from the exposed teeth. Her eyes were half-closed.

Gerry felt a pang of sorrow and guilt and rushed for a towel, scooped Marigold up carefully, wrapped her and cuddled her close. People — and cats — shouldn't have to die alone, she thought. The cat's head hung loosely over her arm.

She got her coffee and a box of tissues and sat in a rocker in the living room talking and crying, telling Marigold what a good cat she was and how much Gerry loved her and how she knew Aunt Maggie had loved her. She leaned over when she said this, so the other cats wouldn't hear her add two words — "the best."

They must have sat there all morning. Around noon, the sun came out and shone into the room and Gerry, having to pee, laid Marigold down on the rug, opening the towel so she could feel the sun on her body. When she got back from the bathroom, it was over.

She knelt on the rug with her hand on Marigold, checking for another breath; lowered her head to listen for the heart beating; marvelled at death, how it extinguished personality so utterly, leaving only memory; and realized the cat had probably only lived through the morning because of feeling the warmth of her lap, hearing the sound of her voice.

The other cats had kept their eyes on things, passing through the room while Marigold still breathed, and now, sniffed at her corpse before moving on.

Gerry made herself another coffee. She wrapped Marigold in the towel but left her on the rug and sat in the rocking chair again. There was no rush. She had all afternoon.

19

"Buried her under the hydrangea. Put a big stone so nobody digs her up by accident."

Prudence wiped her eyes on a tea towel. "Well, I'm very sorry to hear it. Poor little Madame. She was with Maggie for sixteen years. Was probably with her when she died. It's the end of an era. You won't need to cook extra chicken anymore."

Gerry blew her nose into a tissue. "No. And Lightning looks like she's making a move to become top cat. There've been a lot of hissings and threats uttered. And she almost made it through my bedroom door last night."

"Give it time. Give it time. Speaking of which, I think it's time those cat boxes were emptied and scrubbed. You go buy some cat litter and we'll get that done today, plus I'll give that downstairs bathroom a good scrubbing."

Gerry saluted and headed off on her mission.

Lovering was pretty quiet Monday mornings, but she ran into a few people as she went about her errands. They all had a kind word to say about her uncle and she took comfort from that.

It was in a mellow if sad mood that she climbed the bank steps. Doug was just coming out and held the door for her. "Thank you, Doug. How are you?"

He appeared awkward. They both stepped aside as an elderly man entered the bank. "I'm staying with the boys, now, you know."

"Yes, I know. Uh, the cat, Marigold, she died yesterday. I buried her under the hydrangea, you know the one? Her favourite spot."

"Oh, that's too bad. Listen, Gerry, I'm going to be busy with the boys for a while, so — " he paused, looking unhappy.

"Oh, I understand, Doug. You won't have so much time to work around my house. I get it." But do I, Gerry wondered? "Doug, I was meaning to ask you, did you leave the perennials uncut on purpose or — ?"

He nodded. "Maggie liked how it looked with snow on it. Said it was picturesque. There's a bigger cleanup to do in spring but it's worth it, she said."

"So I'll see you there in the spring?"

He looked relieved. "Yeah, yeah. In the spring."

So that's that, she thought a bit sadly, as she entered the bank. When she got home, she unwrapped the paper and string parcel she'd retrieved from her safety deposit box and hung the painting over the sofa in her studio. Then she unloaded the cat litter and piled it outside the bathroom where Prudence laboured. "Prudence, have you got a minute?"

Prudence appeared. "It's not going to clean itself, you know!"

"I know. This way, please." A mystified Prudence stripped off her rubber gloves and followed her back into the studio. Gerry dragged two chairs to face the sofa. "That black and white chunky-looking painting. Look at it."

Prudence looked. "So?"

"It's by Paul-Émile Borduas and I have recently been told that it might fetch a half million dollars at auction."

Prudence was silent. "That one?" she asked incredulously.

"He's a very important French-Canadian artist. Very important."

Prudence stood up. "If you say so. Now can I get back to work?"

"Sit down, Prudence," said an exasperated Gerry. "Don't you see what this means? I can give you and Doug raises. I can insulate the house. I could even — " and here Gerry's self-employed soul disbelieved for a moment. "I could even take a vacation," she concluded in an awestruck tone.

"Good. And I guess it means you can afford to keep those kittens I see Mother carrying across the lawn."

"What?" Gerry rushed to the window. There was Mother, proudly bringing a mewling bundle of black and white up to the cat flap. "But I thought she was fixed!" hollered Gerry, running out of the room.

"Don't ask me how she does it," said Prudence, following. "But she finds them. Aw, aren't they cute?"

"You can keep one," said Gerry, shaking her finger at Mother, proudly licking first one and then another of her five new kittens.

First Cat couldn't settle. No matter how often she ate, she was always terribly hungry. And the last couple of days, nothing she ate stayed down.

Her heart beat uncomfortably fast as she circled next to the young woman. She'd tried to leave earlier that day, leave to do what was necessary, but the woman had brought her back.

Something was happening to her, something important. If only she could get away.

She jumped off the bed. The woman said something to Second Cat, rolled over and went to sleep.

Second Cat looked at First Cat steadily. He knew. She left the room on unsteady legs, passing that other calico outside the bedroom door. She knew too, but First Cat couldn't be bothered with her.

She hopped down the wide staircase, pausing on each step. She hurt all over. Too tired to go outside, she looked for a place.

She passed from room to room, aware of the other cats, prowling or watching. They all knew. They looked away as she passed.

Someone had left the cupboard door open. She went in with a feeling of relief. It was dark. It —

She felt something soft, then felt herself being lifted up. Presently warm liquid dropped on her fur. There was some sound but mostly there was the sound of her own breathing, harsh and slow.

Then she felt the warmth and sound withdraw and she was put on something hard. She felt air on her body and the sun and then —

"Oh, Marigold, you pretty girl. Have you come to be with me?" Familiar arms scooped her up and she felt herself being pressed close to a familiar form. *"I've been waiting for you. You did very well. So helpful. Such a good cat. You always were the best. You know that, don't you?"*

And with similar endearments and a purr of pure joy, woman and cat passed on.

A NOTE ABOUT THE RECIPES

All the recipes are closely guarded family secrets. Prudence only shared them with Gerry because they're cousins. But I'm sure, with a little research, you'll be able to find them yourselves.

A NOTE ABOUT THE PLANTS

The quote on page 147 about the aconite is from *Rodale's Illustrated Encyclopedia of Herbs*, Claire Kowalchuck and William H. Hylton, Editors. Rodale Press, Emmaus, Penn., USA, 1987.

A NOTE ABOUT THE AUTHOR

Born in Montreal and raised in Hudson, Quebec, Louise Carson studied music in Montreal and Toronto, played jazz piano and sang in the chorus of the Canadian Opera Company. Carson has published four books: *Rope*, a blend of poetry and prose set in eighteenth-century Scotland; *Mermaid Road*, a lyrical novella; *A Clearing*, a collection of poetry; and *Executor*, a mystery set in China and Toronto. *The Cat Among Us* is her second mystery.

Her poems appear in literary magazines, chapbooks and anthologies from coast to coast, including *The Best Canadian Poetry 2013*. She's been short-listed in *FreeFall* magazine's annual contest three times, and won a Manitoba Magazine Award. She has presented her work in many public forums, including Hudson's Storyfest 2015, and in Montreal, Ottawa, Toronto, Saskatoon, Kingston and New York City.

She lives in St-Lazare, Quebec, where she writes, teaches music and gardens.